ATTIC LADIES

Gloamin's Gateway

Book One

By D.J. Yates

ISBN 978-1-291-67978-6

Dedicated to the
James George Yates &
and Hilda Francis

With grateful thanks to
Wesley Robinson & Tanya Cook
who made this book possible

Special thanks to
Freya Robinson & Jessica Yates
who were my inspiration
and my partner Norman Robinson

CHAPTER 1

LEDREMAIN

The last of the combine elders arrived. Edmortar and Sapera were now striding up the central aisle of the council chamber. The power of their pace caused their green cloaks to waft behind them and the buckles of their knee high black boots jangled as they walked. There was a loud bang as the guards slammed the large wooden doors shut. A series of locks clicked into place and the chamber was sealed.

Sapera had fond memories of the vast chamber. She remembered playing "hide and hunt" with her brother when she was a child. She had always admired this room. In particular, she admired the beautiful decorative wooden arches, which lined the walls.

Long blue couches were positioned in graduated circular patterns from the floor to the ceiling. The design of the couches was purposeful. It ensured that wherever a council member sat, they could view the senior elders in the inner circle.

They approached the centre of the room. Sapera noticed there were only ten members in attendance. They stood in small

groups talking. She gave Edmortar a bemused glance and communicated with his mind. She considered it unusual that there was such a poor turnout. This was, after all, an emergency meeting. She felt disappointed. People should have made more of an effort to attend.

On their arrival, Edmortar and Sapera were greeted by Ontar. He invited all the council members to be seated. Throughout Sapera's life, Ontar had been the most senior elder. She remembered with great fondness, watching his ceremonial robe day. Sat on her mother's knee, she had been mesmerised by the splendour of the proceedings. The highlight of the ceremony was a silver robe with green velvet piping being placed around Ontar's shoulders. This symbolised his status. Everyone in attendance had stood clapping and dancing to the celebratory music.

Today as she glanced around the room, there was no laughter or music only an air of anxiety and foreboding. There were three other elders dressed in silver robes. The remainder wore the same as Edmortar and Sapera.

The green robed council members felt peculiar. They were unaccustomed to sitting in the senior elders circle. They whispered to each other. The confusion was evident in their faces.

Ontar thanked them all for attending. He requested that they raise their arms and hold hands by interlocking their fingers. He instructed them to close their eyes and open their minds. It was very important that they concentrated. Ontar and the senior robes began chanting. This induced everyone in the circle into a trance. Their faces became expressionless. Their eyelids remained open exposing the whites of their eyes. They spoke the language of the ancient tongue. Ledremain children learnt this in school, however, it was no longer their first language. The words spoken were forceful and rapid. This continued for several minutes. The elders suddenly stopped chanting. The robed circle levitated, approximately one meter from the ground. Gradually, an intense white light swallowed up the room and engulfed the robed figures.

There was a brief moment of silence. The peacefulness was replaced by a crunching noise as if some sort of mechanism had been activated. Sapera could hear stones grinding together and chains clinking. Finally, the clunking of a mechanical device was initiated. It was as if something had been set free. The stone floor in the middle of the circle began to disappear, leaving a black hole beneath their feet. From the darkness, a stone coffin rose up. There was a whoosh sound and the bright light disappeared. Complete silence fell upon the chamber. The stone floor appeared once again and the circle of elders slowly floated to the ground.

The green robes were asked to take their seats. Ontar invited the silver robed elders to join him. The four senior elders took their places one on each side of the coffin. Holding their arms outstretched and their palms facing inwards, they began a whispering chant.

Gradually the coffin lid disappeared and revealed a compartment. The green robed council members shuffled to the edge of their seats. They found the potential content of the coffin intriguing. Unfortunately, their view was obscured by the silver cloaks. In turn, each silver robed elder reached in and took something out of the coffin. When they had all retrieved an object, the stone lid reappeared once again. The silver robed elders placed the four objects on the closed coffin and took their seats. Sapera observed four old wooden boxes. Each had decorative gold trimming around the edges. Secured to the lids of the boxes was a gold key with an elaborately decorated handle. One had an oval shaped yellow sapphire, which glistened as the light reflected upon it. The second was a diamond snowflake design and the third was a sea horse carved from aquamarine. The final key had an emerald in the shape of a leaf.

Everyone looked to Ontar for an explanation. He made it clear that they had very little time. They must all listen carefully to what he was about to tell them. He explained that their civilisation was about to be destroyed. The elders became extremely distressed by his revelation and stood up protesting in disbelief.

Sapera's long brown curly hair began to turn purple. She possessed the gift of mood changing hair. Unfortunately, this had been a help and a hindrance throughout her life. She was anxious and this emotion always presented as the colour purple. Ontar, seeing her distress, appealed for calm. He tried to reassure his council members that plans were in place to ensure their safety.

When everyone had finally composed themselves, he stood up from his chair and walked over to the coffin. Ontar looked upon their anxious faces. He informed them that he would only be distributing a wooden key box to each combine wearing green robes. Two of the silver robed elders raised a fierce objection. They insisted, as senior members, that they were chosen first. The green robed delegates were unaware of the importance of their task and the significance of the boxes. They looked on in astonishment as the debate between the silver robes continued. Ontar, supported by his wife Saira, finally dismissed the objections.

He brought the meeting to order and continued. He had a diversionary plan. The enemy would be hunting for the silver robed elders. Ontar hoped that by giving the key boxes to the green robed combines, he would ensure the key carriers safety. He was optimistic that his plan would not be anticipated. It was a dangerous task and he advised each of the combines to be under no illusion about the risks they would be taking. They may be hunted for the rest of their lives. There would be no recriminations if any one refused this task.

To ensure the complete safety of the boxes and their contents, the green robed council members must escape immediately. They would have to leave everything they had ever known and begin a new life. The boxes and their contents must be hidden safely somewhere far away. The stability of many worlds depended upon their success. Ontar added that it was unlikely that they would return to Ledremain. Each combine was given the opportunity to consider their options. The chosen couples engaged in several minutes of discussion. All agreed to undertake the task entrusted to them. Ontar then distributed a box to each combine. He bid farewell, to each of them, thanking the combines for their loyalty. Placing their hands palm to palm and interlocking their fingers, they then bid each other honour and safe passage.

Some of the combines had started to make their way towards the large wooden doors. They had walked half way along the central isle when they heard shouting outside the chamber. This was followed by scuffling and the sound of swords clashing.

Ontar beckoned the green robes to him. He waved his hand above a stone slab in the senior elders circle. It revealed a set of steps, which led down to a passageway. Hanging on the walls were brightly lit torches. Edmortar waited expecting their senior elder to lead them down the stairway. Ontar shook his head. He explained that he would not be travelling with them. Sapera was shocked to hear this and questioned her father's decision. He kissed her forehead gently. Ontar told her he had to remain to ensure their escape and to protect the rest of the people. Sapera was horrified to hear her mother Saira announce that she would be remaining as well.

Ontar looked at his wife and shook his head. He tried to insist that she left with the others but she would not. He knew better than to argue with her. Although a mild-mannered woman, if she decided on a particular course of action no amount of persuasion would change her decision. Ontar admitted defeat he nodded his head and smiled.

Sapera now refused to go. Saira put her arms around her daughter. As they held each other, she whispered in Sapera's ear. "Your children need you, you must leave." Sapera knew her mother was right. Her place was with her husband and her children.

Ontar hugged his daughter once again and asked his son in law to take good care of her. Edmortar put his arm firmly around his wife's shoulders and walked towards the steps leading to the passageway. Sapera looked at her husband and shook her head. She could not leave her father and mother. She had decided that she would stay and fight at her parent's side.

Ontar could see his daughter's red defiant hair and instructed Edmortar to take her. Edmortar picked Sapera up and carried her down the steps. She struggled to break free, tearfully imploring her mother and father to go with them. Ontar smiled reassuringly and then, waving his arm over the passageway entrance, it slowly closed. The council members looked up through the small opening and sadly watched until the passage way was sealed. Edmortar put his arm around Sapera's shoulder she buried her head in his chest and sobbed. They followed the others along the passageway, carrying their boxes under their cloaks. All of a sudden they heard muffled sounds above them. Fearing discovery, they sadly quickened their pace. They were devastated to leave their elders. However, their priority had to be the safety of their families and the protection of the boxes.

The doors of the council chambers burst open. The four remaining elders looked sharply towards the sound and saw grey shadowed creatures pouring into the room. Ontar quickly realised they were out-numbered. The creatures scrambled over the couches. They moved very quickly towards the centre of the chamber and would be upon the elders very soon.

The four silver robed elders stood back to back in the inner circle. They drew their ketarian blades; each sword was individually fashioned to suit the hand of its warrior. The elder stood on the right of Ontar and facing the central isle was his wife Saira. The silver robe with his back to Saira had thick tattooed arms. His combine stood next to him with her back to Ontar. Saira and Ontar had rarely spoken to the combines who now fought beside them, but felt honoured to stand with them today. With their ketarians held high, they prepared to fight.

Suddenly Ontar saw several silver robed councillors enter through the doorway. Ontar smiled and relaxed his shoulders, reinforcements had arrived. He touched his wife's arm to reassure her and she sighed with relief. Floods of emotion rushed through her body. The reinforcements gave a glimmer of hope. The likelihood of seeing her daughter and grandchildren once again was now a possibility.

At that moment, Saira fell to the floor and began crying out in pain. Ontar was confused, had his wife been wounded? The shadow creatures had not reached them yet. He wondered if perhaps a spear or a knife had injured her. Ontar quickly knelt down on one knee and cradled Saira in his arms. He spoke gently to her trying to determine the cause of her pain. He turned her face towards him. Ontar watched as the colour drained from her beautiful green eyes and became completely grey. He knew this appearance only too well. Her mind had been manipulated.

Only people with exceptional powers could perform this act. It was a skill perfected by the most senior elders. He looked to the silver robes standing close to him for help and support. The tattooed silver robed man grinned. His eyes then turned black and became transfixed upon Ontar. Suddenly, Ontar felt horrendous pain in his head. He clutched his skull trying to ease his suffering and finally slumped forward across Saira's body. He had suspected treachery for some time but had been unable to identify any traitor within their midst. It would seem his enemy had been so close for a long time. Saira took a sharp intake of breath, Ontar kissed her cheek.

He struggled to his feet and tried not to shout out in pain. Facing the tattooed traitor, he raised his ketarian. Ontar felt a sharp pain pass through his head. It was unbearable and he found himself on the ground once again.

He reached for Saira's hand and gripped it tightly. Looking up, he could see six silver robed elders had formed a circle around them. Their eyes were black. Their minds began probing and feeling their way through his thoughts. Ontar was unable to tolerate the pain any longer and collapsed into a state of unconsciousness.

Sheathing their ketarians, the tattooed traitor and his accomplices strode towards the council chamber doors. They marched through the sea of shadow creatures that parted to allow them through. The tattooed silver robed elder instructed some of the Gloamin creatures to bring Ontar and Saira. They did as their master instructed and the creatures dragged their two captives, who were powerless to resist, from the chamber.

The other creatures went in search of the wooden boxes, which they would retrieve by any means possible.

CHAPTER 2

ATTIC LADIES

'SILVERGLOMIN ROAD, ENGLAND, THIRTEEN YEARS LATER.'

Freya stood in the corner of the kitchen leaning against the work surface. She wore earphones and her eyes were transfixed on her Ipad. She was oblivious to her surroundings. Mrs Jenkins was beginning to get a little cross with her daughter. This would be the third time she had asked Freya to take the breakfast tray to the ladies and there was still no response. It was difficult to attract Freya's attention when she was lost in Ipad world. Exasperated, her mother picked up the tray from the table and waved it in front of Freya's face.

Freya removed her earphones and had a surprised 'what's all the fuss about' look on her face. Freya protested that she was just about to do it. Mrs Jenkins then repeated one of Freya's favourite sayings "I was just gonna. They'll put that on your grave stone". Freya had turned away from her mother and was mimicking her mum's speech. Placing the Ipad down on the work surface she turned to face her mother smiled and took hold of the breakfast tray. Freya then proceeded to huff and tut her way out of the kitchen.

Mrs Jenkins continued rushing around cooking breakfast and making the packed lunches. They were running late, as usual. School mornings were always stressful. She allowed her thoughts to drift to this time tomorrow, it would be Saturday and she would be nestled under her duvet having a well-deserved lie-in.

She snapped out of her daydream on hearing the high-pitched squeal of the smoke detector. Mrs Jenkins began frantically wafting the tea towel at the small white box attached to the ceiling. She had been so distracted she had not noticed the toast sending up smoke signals.

Freya could hear the commotion coming from the kitchen. She stood at the bottom of the stairs looking up at the banister, which twisted through the three- storey building. She felt weary just looking at the number of stairs she would have to climb. Her mission was to ensure the boiled eggs did not topple out of their holders again. She'd had to chase them down a flight of stairs the day before. The eggs were so badly broken the ladies, who never complain, had commented on the poor presentation of the food. The smell of the hot buttered toast reminded her stomach that she hadn't eaten yet. Resting the tray on the banister at the base of the stairs, Freya dipped her finger in the pot of her mother's homemade strawberry jam. Just something to keep me going she thought.

Heaving a huge sigh, she began her ascent. In the past, it had seemed strange that nobody knew why the ladies were living in the attic. Where they had come from was a mystery. When asked, her mother would simply say, "They are just there and we are glad of it".

Freya finally reached the third floor she walked over to the attic door and knocked twice. Two elderly ladies appeared in the doorway and invited her in. Their small gentle faces were always happy to see visitors. They were never grumpy, sad, or angry. It was strange that she never saw the ladies leave the attic but she had her suspicions that they did.

The smallest of the ladies was called Jess. She had hair the colour of snow with tight ringlet curls just touching her shoulder. Her face was tiny. She had bright green eyes and high cheekbones. Jess was petite. She always wore an artist's style blouse over a long blue skirt, which touched the floor. She loved paint and was very talented.

Hilda was tall and thin. She had long dark grey hair, which she wore in a bun at the back of her head secured with two chopsticks. She had a thin face with beautiful dark green eyes. Hilda always wore bright patterned trousers and a brilliant white blouse. Freya called her the oracle. She always knew the best thing to do, whatever the situation.

Freya placed the breakfast tray on the table by the window at the far end of the attic. She kissed the ladies goodbye and shut the door behind her.

A commanding voice sounded from the bottom of the stairs. It was Mrs Jenkins. If Freya didn't get a move on, she was going to be late. Stretching one leg over the banister, she slid down the three flights of stairs. She jumped off at the bottom and raced into the kitchen.

Her brother Wesley sat at the table tucking into his breakfast. He was four years older than Freya and attended Sixth Form College studying for his 'A' levels. He had blonde hair and green eyes. Freya's friends thought he was very good looking. She had to admit he was a lovely brother. Wes was kind and thoughtful and was always a shoulder to cry on when she was upset.

Freya heard the doorbell, it was her best friend Chloe. She bent down and kissed Wes on his cheek. Whilst saying goodbye, her hand located a piece of toast on his plate and she managed to snatch it despite Wesley's objections. Mrs Jenkins then began to give the second speech of the morning "If you got up earlier and didn't play on that Ipad..." Freya did not stop to listen. She had kissed her mum good bye and was already in the entrance hall before the speech was finished. She swung her bag over her shoulder and slammed the front door behind her. As she did so she could hear her mother shout, "don't slam the front door" but it was too late.

The ladies sat in front of the attic window enjoying their breakfast. They had a marvellous view and were able to observe all the activities in Silverglomin Road. Freya seemed so happy walking to school with her best friend. Chloe had met the ladies several times and they were pleased she was such a good friend to Freya. Wesley left the house about fifteen minutes later with two of his friends. He had recently passed his driving test and had bought a second hand car. The ladies watched as the three boys climbed into the mini and drove away. Mr and Mrs Jenkins left a short time after Wes. They looked up to the attic window and waved to the ladies before pulling out of the driveway.

The house was quiet once again. Having finished their breakfast, they began clearing away their dirty dishes.

All at once, the attic became very dark. It was as if a black cloud had settled outside the window and was blocking out the daylight. There was a sudden flash of lightning. It was so bright the ladies were forced to put their hands up to protect their eyes. When they lowered their hands, they noticed two old wooden chairs had appeared in the centre of the room. The chairs were joined together but faced in opposite directions. Each had two arms and four legs. The wooden seats did not look particularly comfortable. Hilda stared vacantly as if her mind was far away. Jess was worried she tried to speak to her several times but there was no response. She had little option but to wait.

It was about thirty seconds later when Hilda finally became aware of her surroundings once again. Jess was curious to know what was going on. Hilda explained that a voice had spoken directly to her mind. Something was very wrong and somebody needed their help. The voice had instructed them to sit down on the wooden chairs and very soon things would become clear. They did as they were requested. Cautiously sitting down on the chairs, they were uncertain of what to expect. They didn't have long to wait. As they were fastening the safety belts attached to the back of the chairs, the seats began to vibrate. The ladies firmly gripped the arms. They gently rose into the air, a little way initially and then higher until they were about two meters off the ground. Coloured smoke swirled around the room.

The chairs started spinning slowly around in a circle. They then rapidly increased acceleration, until they reached such a tremendous speed, that the ladies heads were pushed back in to the headrests. Their faces looked distorted as their cheeks rippled against the G-force. Suddenly, the chairs came to an abrupt halt. Jess's chair broke away and turned one hundred and eighty degrees anti-clockwise and the chairs then re-joined. They now sat side by side facing in the same direction. In one swift movement, the chair backs jerked downward and were now parallel with the floor. The ladies lay facing upwards towards the ceiling. It was as if they were about to be launched from a rocket. As they looked upwards, they could see the sky picture Jess had painted on the ceiling. Hilda noticed that Jess's attention to detail was amazing. She had never really appreciated how beautiful the picture was. They sat in their chairs, anticipating something amazing was about to happen. The chairs moved upwards towards the painting and then dropped back down towards the floor. This happened on two occasions. All of a sudden they began shaking from side to side and then headed straight towards the ceiling. Both ladies let out a scream "ahhhhhhhh!"

When they opened their eyes, they were amazed to find they had travelled through the ceiling painting and were now flying through the sky. Frantically they checked each other for cuts and bruises. Fortunately, they were unscathed. The ladies smiled at each other and then laughed with relief. Up and up they travelled. It was exciting. They found themselves flying over green fields, small streams, and mountains with beautiful waterfalls.

The ladies enjoyed the peacefulness of the blue skies. Apart from the wind rushing past their ears, they wouldn't have known they were moving. It was cool but the sun's warm glow ensured they were comfortable. The ladies hadn't experienced being out of the attic for a very long time and they wanted to savour every moment. The smell of the clear crisp air, the warmth of the sun and the beautiful vibrant colours refreshed their memories. These influences would be an inspiration for Jess's future art works when they return to the attic.

They approached clouds, which appeared to be camouflaging sky buildings. The ladies could see the outline of a palace. The chairs came to a graceful halt. Unbuckling their belts, they stepped onto a footpath. The path was made of white marble and contained sparkling silver flecks which shone beautifully in the sun's rays. Smiling at each other, they knew they had trodden this route before. They had only walked half-way up the path when the door of the palace opened. A tall man wearing a green hooded robe stepped out and came striding towards them.

The ladies greeted their old friend Romain. They were very pleased to see him again after all this time and hoped he was well. As they embraced, he kissed them both on each cheek. Now standing between them, the ladies gazed up at him.

He was a distinguished looking man; very tall and slim, with white hair and piercing green eyes. He put his arms around their shoulders and they continued along the path. The ladies chatted about their amazing journey and thanked him for inviting them out of the attic. Romain was also glad to see them once again. However, he wished they were meeting under different circumstances. Something terrible had happened and he hoped they would be able to work together to put things right.

On reaching the door of the palace, they walked into the grand entrance hall. It was a white circular room with a pale blue and white checked floor. An orchestra dressed in white top hat and tails played classical music on a high balcony. A large fountain stood in the centre of the room. The colour and the size of the water in the fountain changed to the mood and pace of the music. It was so beautiful they couldn't resist admiring it for a few moments. After a short while, they sensed that Romain was keen to move on.

He escorted them through a doorway and into a large room. Looking up, they could see an arch shaped entrance positioned in the upper part of the wall. They turned to ask Romain about the curious opening but he wasn't there. The ladies were astonished to see Romain standing in mid-air. He invited them to join him. He was climbing an invisible staircase. They hesitated to follow him. Jess tentatively started touching the bottom stair just to reassure herself there was something there. When they had mustered up the courage, they cautiously followed him. It was a strange feeling walking up a staircase they couldn't physically see. Every step they made was exaggerated. The ladies were concerned they may stumble and fall. However as they became more familiar with the stairs, they used their intuition to guide their feet. Eventually it became automatic, as if they were accustomed to climbing the steps every day.

When they finally reached the top of the staircase, they found themselves in a narrow, white walled corridor. There were beautiful bright blue eye shaped lights equally spaced along the walls. Each light became dimmer as they walked past it, which gave the illusion that the lights were winking at them. This made the ladies smile. They appreciated Romain's sense of humour.

At the end of the corridor was a gigantic door covered in red velvet. It was three meters high and at least a meter thick. In the middle of the door was a huge gold handle. Romain turned the handle, he began to push the heavy door with the help of the ladies. They laughed as they reminisced on how they had done this when they were children. Romain nodded and smiled.

On entering the room, the ladies had forgotten how spacious it was, they saw it contained comfortable white couches and large blue armchairs. The chairs were positioned around a roaring open fire, which was in the centre of the room. Romain gestured to the ladies to sit down and make themselves comfortable. They glanced around and noticed a great number of exquisitely designed windows.

They were all different shapes and sizes. Romain stood in front of the largest window which was arch shaped and contained an assortment of coloured glass. It extended from the floor to the ceiling and was quite magnificent. He waved his hand and a swirling mist consumed Romain and the window.

When the mist cleared, it revealed a dark and distressing scene. The ladies walked towards the window and were horrified at what they saw. Six very young children were huddled together crying. They appeared cold and uncared for.

It was a very emotive scene; the ladies were saddened to see children suffering in this way. Their wrists were tied and they were all attached to a long piece of rope. At the other end of the length of rope was a sinister grey shadow. The shadow was dragging the children along a mountainous path in a strange land. The children were cowering, obviously terrified of the creature.

The ladies were appalled by this horrific scene and could not understand who would do such a dreadful thing to children. Romain explained that the children had been taken from the world of Daluce a few weeks previously and despite their extreme efforts, they had not physically or mentally been able to locate them. Unfortunately their powers of telepathy had not fully developed. Romain did not know why the children had been taken or where they had been taken. However, he did know that one of the children would play a very important part in the ladies future destiny.

Romain gave the creatures a name. They were known as Gloamins. He was concerned that not only had they taken the children, unfortunately, they had stolen one of the four life keys. The life keys formed the very foundation of their society. Romain knew the Gloamins did not have the intelligence to organise these acts. He impressed upon the ladies that only someone in a position of great power would be able to orchestrate these events. He had been unable to determine who was responsible but felt there was an undercurrent of manipulation and mischief. He stressed that the definitive priority would be the safe return of the children. The missing key would not initially present an immediate problem. However, if the Gloamins were to discover the hiding place of the other three keys, it would be catastrophic. The Gloamins would then have direct access to the attic and ultimately to earth and its inhabitants. The ladies nodded in agreement. They knew they must find the children and ensure the key was returned. It was a huge responsibility but one Romain hoped the ladies were willing to undertake. He stressed it was vital that centuries of stability continued to be maintained.

CHAPTER 3

FREYA

Freya walked into the classroom in time for registration. It was the usual Friday morning. Everyone was noisily talking about their plans for the weekend. Some of the girls sat on top of the desks using their mobile phones. The boys talked about football or flicked each other with rulers.

Freya put her backpack on the desk and flopped down onto her chair. A strange feeling began to wash over her. She felt a cold chill run through her bones and the hairs on her arms were standing on end. She sat with a faraway look in her eyes. Something was wrong. Chloe who had been chattering away suddenly noticed her friend wasn't responding to her question. She became concerned and asked Freya what was troubling her, she seemed to be in a world of her own. Freya continued to stare blankly. It was only when her hand was tapped by a concerned Chloe that she became aware of her surroundings once again. Chloe had a worried look on her face. Freya laughed and explained that she had simply been daydreaming. Her friend was not convinced, she knew when Freya was lying. Chloe was a fair haired girl with big brown eyes and serious freckles. She was an orphan. Her parents were killed in a car crash when she was a toddler. She had no living relatives. Fostering had never really worked out for her and she continued to live in a children's home. Since living in the home, she had acquired a large number of brothers and sisters. They drove her crazy at times but she wouldn't have it any other way.

The girls had remained friends since their first day of nursery school. They normally spent every weekday, most weekends and virtually all of the school holidays together. However, this weekend Chloe was going on a short break with the staff from the children's home. They would be camping and spending two days at a theme park. Chloe would be texting Freya on Sunday morning to arrange the time and place for meeting up on Sunday afternoon. Fortunately, they had just finalised their plans when Miss Higgins entered the classroom.

The class settled down and became quiet almost immediately. She had been their form teacher since their first day in secondary school and would remain with her class until their final year. Miss Higgins was brilliant. They couldn't have asked for a better mentor. If anyone was troubled, she would be there to listen and give support. She was in her late twenties, extremely pretty with piercing blue eyes, blonde bobbed hair, average height, very slim and always looked stunning in her designer clothes. She had recently become engaged. Her wedding date was set for eleven months time and she would announce each morning how many sleeps until her wedding day. The boys would groan every time she mentioned it. The girls however would become excited and were intrigued when she talked about the wedding plans. Today she wore a smart black trouser suit and a pink blouse with very fine black stripes. She looked fabulous. Her shoes were always high. Freya's mum would never let her have high heels. Her mother insisted on flat footwear. Although she loved her baseball boots, she would love a heel on her shoes. Miss Higgins told the class there were 330 sleeps until her wedding. She then laughed as the boys groaned. After calling the register, she proceeded to go through numerous announcements. The final piece of information was disappointing.

There had been a flood in the dance and drama studio. Some people in the class would have to go to the library for the whole day to do coursework. Unfortunately, Freya was one of those people. Having completed most of her coursework, she didn't want to sit in the library all day.

Once again, a strange sensation came over her. It was a feeling of impending doom. Something was terribly wrong and her sixth sense told her it concerned the attic ladies. The feeling had been momentary but long enough to unsettle her. Freya made a decision. She was going to skip the library and go home! Chloe agreed to cover for her during the morning and they would meet up at afternoon registration. She was so glad they were friends, they could always rely on each other whatever the crisis.

Freya managed to slip out of school without anyone seeing her. She didn't have to wait very long to catch her bus to the high street and from there it was just a ten minute walk to the house. She arrived home and ran up the three flights of stairs to the attic. When she finally reached the top of the house, she was out of breath. She took a few seconds to lean on the banister before she knocked on the attic door. There was no immediate reply. She tried again and knocked a little louder. There was still no response. Freya was now becoming very concerned, the ladies had always answered a knock at their door. She feared her suspicion was correct.

Freya pushed the door open, she wanted to be wrong and hoped she would surprise them. To her dismay, the room was empty and the ladies were missing. Freya had never been in the attic without the ladies being present. She looked around the room. Oddly, the breakfast tray containing dirty dishes had been left on the table in front of the window. The ladies had always washed their dishes and normally left them stacked neatly on the tray.

Freya left the attic and began searching for the ladies. She explored every floor of the house and investigated every room. Finally, she ended her search in the kitchen. Sitting down on one of the kitchen stools, she began biting her lip and wondering what to do next.

Her stomach was rumbling. The kitchen clock told her it was morning break time. She decided she would think better on a full stomach and began mooching through the fridge and the food cupboards. Making her choice, she switched on the kettle and made herself a pot noodle. With her morning snack in one hand and a plastic fork in the other, she raced up to the attic taking the stairs two at a time. Flinging the door open, she expected to surprise the ladies but there was still no sign of life. Freya sat down at the table in front of the window and ate her noodles. When she had finished eating, she turned around to face the room.

She smiled as she thought about the ladies and their disagreements regarding the colour scheme for decorating the attic. Hilda resolved the dispute. Her proposal was for Jess to paint a different themed picture on each of the attic walls.

The blue wall had an ocean scene. It was vast and contained all sorts of sea creatures. There were beautiful coloured fish, sea horses, starfish, a school of dolphins, and two whales. At the rear of the picture, the water became a darker blue and shark fins were visible. Freya squinted to view the very back of the painting. There appeared to be a grey smudge on the picture. She stood up from her chair and walked over to examine the painting more closely. Freya noticed it wasn't a smudge at all. It was a creepy shadowy shaped figure partially hidden behind the rocks. Freya shuddered, she wondered what Jess was thinking, putting that in her painting.

Freya moved over to the green wall. This was a forest scene with green fields and beautiful flowers. There were vibrant coloured birds nesting in tall trees. A family of deer stood in a sunny clearing whilst rabbits jumped around them. Towards the rear of the painting, there were two bicycles leaning against a tree and a small fluffy dog lying on the ground with a stick in his mouth. In the distance was a beautiful cascading waterfall. The water bounced off several rock ledges on its way down into a deep turquoise lagoon. Rocks and lilies surrounded the water. Above the waterfall was a cave and another shadowy figure lurked in the mouth of the cavern.

On the right hand wall, closest to the window was a desert scene. The golden sand looked so real it gave the illusion that you could run your fingers through it. In the distance were three pyramids. Each had a different sized jewel at the top. The middle pyramid had the largest and the sun shone through the centre of it generating beams of light onto the sand. In front of the pyramids was a train of camels led by a man in long striped robes and a ghutra on his head. Behind the camels were two boys. They were dressed in long white robes. They also wore ghutras. To the far right of the picture was a sultan's palace. Its tall towers were crowned in gold, which glistened brightly in the sun's rays. Soldiers patrolled the walkways between the towers. They carried wooden staffs and shiny silver scimitars, which hung around their waist. Their tunics were bright red and they wore shiny black boots and had black turbans around their heads. The face of a beautiful girl appeared at a tiny window in the tower. She looked very sad. In front of the palace was a crowded market place. People were busy buying many different types of household goods. Outside the city walls there was a small oasis surrounded by palm trees. There were a great number of camels drinking at the water pool and men in long white robes sat around chatting. Lurking behind one of the palm trees was a grey shadowed silhouette.

The white wall felt cold when Freya touched it. At the front of the picture were six dogs pulling a sleigh through deep snow. Seated in the sleigh was a man, a woman and a little girl. They were all huddled together under a blanket. Towards the back of the picture were high snow covered grey mountains. To the right of the painting was a large group of penguins. They were standing together with their backs to a snow blizzard, which had whipped up behind them. Roaming in the distance was a family of polar bears.

Down in a deep valley Jess had painted a beautiful quaint village. It was nestled against the towering mountains. The little wooden houses had twinkling lights in their tiny windows and white smoke puffed out of the chimneys. The people walking around the streets wore fur coats and hats and appeared to be battling against high winds. As they walked across the entrance to an alley, they seemed unaware of a shadowed figure lurking there.

Freya walked over to the attic window. She looked out onto the road wondering where the ladies could be. She would give them five more minutes then she would phone her mother. She knew she would be in trouble for not being at school, but she was far more concerned about the fate of the ladies.

The attic ladies were now ready to leave the cloud palace. They said goodbye to Romain and returned to the wooden chairs at the end of the glistening pathway. Before they could begin their search for the children and the key, they would have to return to the attic and gather some essentials for the journey.

Freya looked up at the ceiling. It was a beautiful powder blue and white fluffy clouds were scattered throughout the picture. The sun shone warmly .There were flocks of different types of birds flying in formation across the sky. In the distance there was a castle made of clouds and a rather wise looking man stood at the entrance in a green hooded robe. She couldn't see any shadowy figures in the picture. It was calm and relaxing.

Freya couldn't wait any longer. She had to let someone know that the ladies were missing. She walked over to the door and was about to leave the attic when she heard a strange noise. Freya looked for the origin of the sound but it was difficult to locate. The noise became louder and louder and she watched as coloured smoke spiralled from the ceiling and began swirling around the attic.

Freya could see something emerging from the ceiling. She couldn't believe her eyes. It was Jess and Hilda. They were spinning around on two old wooden chairs. A trail of coloured smoke whirled around them. Freya was glued to the spot. She wanted to run but her legs were like lead. She was frightened but couldn't turn away from the strange sight that lay before her. The chairs finally stopped spinning and landed in the middle of the attic floor. When the smoke cleared, Freya stared at the ladies who were now sat opposite her. She was in shock and began uttering words such as "How did you?" and "Where did you?"

Jess undid her safety belt, got up from her seat and walked over to Freya. She put her arm around Freya's shoulder and sat her down in the comfy arm chair. Jess then pulled up a stool and sat opposite her. Hilda walked across the room and joined them. Both ladies tried to reassure Freya that she shouldn't be frightened by what she had seen. The ladies apologised that they didn't have time to explain what was going on, but they had a treacherous mission to embark upon and they had to leave immediately.

They moved over to the other side of the room, away from Freya. They began discussing whether they should take Freya with them, this would allow them time to explain everything to her. Hilda doubted Freya's maturity to take on such an adventure. Jess however was more optimistic. Both ladies knew that there would never be an ideal time for Freya to be ready for such a challenge. Jess believed with their support and guidance it could be achievable. The ladies were aware that they needed to make a decision quickly. Realising they couldn't abandon Freya in this confused state; they agreed to put their proposition to her.

Hilda disappeared into the bedroom to organise provisions for the journey. Jess asked Freya if she trusted them. There was no doubt in Freya's mind. She answered by nodding her head. Jess then briefly explained about the missing children. Freya didn't understand and thought that the ladies should pass the information onto the police. Jess assured her that the police would never be in a position to help. Freya was very confused but allowed her to continue. Jess invited Freya to join them but stipulated she would have to do exactly as she was told. She stressed that children's lives would be depending upon them. They had to get things right the first time, there would be no second chances!

Freya was bewildered by this very brief explanation. She had many questions whizzing around in her mind but quickly realised that discussions were not an option and that enlightenment would come later. Freya was thrilled to be asked and promised to do as she was told. She would have to leave a note for her mum and dad. Freya smiled. She had a plan. She could tell her parents she was staying overnight at Chloe's. Freya was sure she hadn't told her mum about Chloe's weekend away at the theme park.

Hilda was almost ready to go and was getting a little anxious. She shouted from the bedroom and told Freya to get changed. Hilda reminded her there wasn't to be lot of fuss about what she was wearing she was to pick something sensible. Freya nodded, ran out of the attic down the stairs, and charged into her bedroom.

She changed out of her school uniform as quickly as possible. It crossed her mind that the ladies may leave without her and were simply humouring her. Therefore, hurrying, she put on her skinny jeans, t-shirt and hooded sweater. She stood looking at herself in the mirror her t-shirt was a perfect match for her green eyes. Freya was undecided about her choice of jeans and was about to change them when she remembered what she had been told, "No fuss". "Okay that will do", she thought to herself. Now what should she do with her hair? It was waist length. Freya decided to leave it loose and put a hair band around her wrist. She could tie it back later if she needed to. Emptying the books from her school bag, she now had space for her supplies. She threw in a few essentials her toothbrush, toothpaste, pyjamas, clean underwear and a spare t-shirt.

Suddenly, there was a flash of bright light in her bedroom. Fearing the ladies may be leaving without her, she raced up to the attic and flung the door open. She was relieved to see the ladies were still there.

Freya began to ask if she had packed the right things. She stopped short and began staring at the ladies. Jess and Hilda were standing by the window. Freya's only thought was "what are they wearing"! Thankfully, she hadn't expressed her dismay out loud. Hilda was dressed in leggings, a crop top, and a hooded sweatshirt. Her long grey hair was tied back in a ponytail. Jess wore black leggings, denim shorts and a cream jumper. On their feet, they both wore a pair of expensive trainers. Freya couldn't help wondering why the ladies were dressed like teenagers. She didn't want to be rude and hoped the distain in her face didn't show. She debated whether to comment on their clothing choices but thought better of it. With everything else that was going on, this fashion disaster was going to be the least of their problems.

Freya was wondering what the next part of the plan involved when Jess, who now stood in the middle of the room, asked Freya to join her. Freya noticed three wooden chairs. They were lined up across the middle of the floor facing the attic window. Jess asked Freya to sit down on the middle chair. The ladies then sat either side of her. Hilda gave a few basic instructions for riding the chairs. Freya was to fasten her safety belt and hold onto the arms of the chair tightly.

They all sat in silence. Freya rested her hands on the arms of the chair. She was feeling quite brave but as soon as the chair started to vibrate and lift off the floor, she panicked and gripped the wooden arms tightly. The chairs separated and formed a circle. Freya and the ladies were now facing inward and began to move around slowly in an anti-clockwise direction. Freya relaxed her grip on the chair. This isn't bad at all, she thought to herself. The chairs were only separated for a few seconds and then came back together again. They were in a line once again facing the attic window. They remained floating in the air but were perfectly still.

The ladies looked at each other wondering what to expect next. The chairs began to vibrate once again and started twisting and turning around the room like a snake. After lapping the room twice, the chairs stopped and hovered. Suddenly Freya and the ladies were tipped upside down. Hilda and Jess's chairs began spinning in a continual forward motion. Freya's chair started rotating backwards repeatedly. She began screaming and protesting that she didn't like it and asked the ladies to stop the ride. She wanted to get off! They explained that they didn't have any control over the chairs.

Freya normally avoided rides at the fair ground that spun around. They made her feel sick. Hoping this wouldn't go on for much longer, she began to worry that she may embarrass herself by vomiting. The ladies tried to reassure Freya that it would be over soon. The three chairs then began spinning backwards and turned repeatedly in a three hundred and sixty degrees motion. After revolving several times the chairs came to an abrupt halt upside down. They separated and formed a circle facing each other and began spinning clockwise. Freya kept repeating that they were going to fall out.

One by one, the chairs became right side up and, once again, they were in a line side by side. The attic window was now to their right. Freya raised her voice above the sound of the vibrating chairs. She had noticed that although the chairs had stopped spinning, the attic room was now turning around them. She found this slightly alarming. The green wall appeared to be getting very close to them, as it passed by. She worried that they might collide with it. Freya wondered if there was a steering wheel or some sort of lever that they could use to steer away from the wall or simply stop the ride. Feeling underneath her seat, she tried to find something that would help them. To her disappointment, she found nothing. Her next suggestion was to jump off the chairs. She was very concerned for the ladies safety and worried that they were going to get hurt.

The room continued to spin around them. Each time it spun, the green wall came closer. Suddenly the chairs picked up tremendous speed and Freya's head was pushed backwards. It felt as if they must have been travelling at least one hundred miles an hour. Looking straight ahead, she could see they were on a collision course with the green wall. Freya frantically tried to undo her safety belt and advised the ladies to do the same but it was impossible to open. Freya could feel the air rushing past her cheeks and her hair felt out of control. She screamed and shut her eyes. Grabbing hold of Jess's arm, she buried her head into her shoulder and continued to scream. With one eye open, she watched as the chairs travelled straight at the wall. Just before they collided, Freya shut her eyes tightly and braced herself for the impact. However, the chairs didn't crash. They simply floated weightlessly through the picture as if in slow motion. Freya's eyes remained tightly shut until the chairs finally touched down. She was very relieved to feel solid ground beneath her feet once again.

A female voice spoke to Freya telling her they had arrived safely. The voice seemed familiar but it didn't sound quite like

Jess or Hilda. She opened her eyes and turned her head to the right and then to the left. She discovered the ladies were not there, two teenage girls were in their place. Freya frantically snapped open her safety belt. She jumped up and turned to look at the two strangers who now occupied Jess and Hilda's chairs. The girl with the blonde curly hair spoke first. She told Freya not to be frightened. She explained that, although their appearance was different, they truly were her attic ladies.

She stared at both of them looking deep into their green eyes. Freya smiled. She recognised that familiar glint that she had become accustomed too. However, how could this be possible? She wasn't sure she actually believed what she was seeing. The fact that two teenage girls had replaced Jess and Hilda was bizarre. She laughed to herself. Now she understood about the ladies peculiar choice of clothes. However, she still didn't understand how, or what, was going on. Jess tried to elaborate. The girl's true names were Hassina and Jalay. Apart from changing their names, they were the same ladies she had known all of her life. There was no reason for her to be afraid or suspicious. Whatever their appearance, their assignment was still the same. They needed to find the missing children. Freya wanted to know more. She began asking many questions. Hassina explained that they had been transmogrified many years ago. They were forced to live in their disguises for their own protection and the defence of many other civilisations. The attic is responsible for guarding many secrets. When they entered the picture Jess had painted, they became themselves once again. This explanation was way above Freya's understanding. They all agreed it was going to be some time before she would be able to digest all of this strange information.

The girls were very pleased that Freya had come to join them and they promised to take care of her. Freya shook her head and laughed. She couldn't believe she was going to be continuing with this crazy adventure.

CHAPTER 4

GYM

The chairs had landed in a field surrounded by trees. It resembled the picture on the attic wall. Lying on the ground was a small white dog. Jalay introduced the beautiful ball of fluff as Gym. He briefly glanced up at Freya with his big blue eyes and winked. Gym then turned his attention back to the stick he had been gnawing. He was trying to hang onto it with his front paws but was struggling to keep control. Freya thought he was adorable. She knelt down and began to stroke his deep fluffy coat. She could tell he liked the attention. His long tail began to swish back and forth. Freya asked if this was their guard dog and if he was more ferocious than he looked. Hassina became very serious and informed her that nothing would be quite what it seems in this world. They should be on their guard and expect the unexpected. This piece of information troubled Freya considerably.

The girls walked across the clearing and made their way towards a footpath on the far side. Freya walked shoulder to shoulder with Jalay and constantly looked around surveying the area. In the event of any danger, she would be prepared to run.

As they approached the path, Freya could see three bicycles leaning against a tree. Jalay confirmed Freya's suspicions; this would be their transportation. She distinctly remembered there had been only two bikes in the attic painting and they were both red. Hassina laughed. When Freya had left the attic to change her clothes Jess had quickly painted another bicycle in Freya's favourite colour purple. Freya hugged Jalay and thanked her. She turned to face her bicycle and quickly took a step backwards. Gym was standing in front of her. He was the same size as her bike. She looked at the girls in disbelief. Jess explained that Gym was an Expandasor and he had the ability to increase or decrease his size at will. Freya was now a little uneasy. She was not a fan of big dogs because of an unfortunate incident as a small child. She cautiously edged her way around the dog keeping her eyes on him as she made her way to her bicycle. When they had determined that everyone was ready, they set off on their journey. Hassina led the way, followed closely by Freya. Jalay was at the rear. Hassina and Jalay began pedalling with no problems at all. However, Freya hadn't ridden a bike for such a long time. She wavered all over the path making a variety of noises. She almost crashed on several occasions. Fortunately, she managed to put her feet down on the ground just in time to save herself. The girls tried to be supportive but found Freya's antics extremely funny. They were, however, careful not to let Freya see their amusement.

Freya found the whole experience unbelievable. She was blown away by the idea that they were actually in a picture. Unfortunately, Freya kept repeating her fascination much to the annoyance of the girls. Hassina tried to change the topic of conversation and began talking about the weather. She commented on the beautiful sunny day and how warm the sun felt on her face. Freya compared it to the weather at home. She then became excited again about having nice weather in a picture. The girls were exasperated with her and told her that she didn't have to remind them where they were any more. She finally got the message.

The path wound its way through woodland for several hours. The cycling made them realise how unfit they were. Poor Gym who had been running beside them looked tired and thirsty. The girls decided to stop and give him a drink. Hassina produced a large bowl from her backpack. She poured in some of her bottled water. Gym lapped it up, drinking the bowl dry. Jalay took out a packet of moist tissues and gave a couple to Freya and Hassina. They all wiped their faces and the back of their necks hoping it would cool them down. After having a cold drink from the cool bag, they started their journey once again.

Freya looked down at the pedals as she wanted to make sure she had her feet in the correct position. When she looked up, she noticed Gym had shrunk. He was now the size of a Labrador puppy. Hassina picked him up and placed him in the basket on the front of her bike. She felt it would be kinder to give him a lift. He loved the wind blowing in his face and kept snapping and trying to eat the breeze. Freya thought he looked so cute.

They had only travelled for a further twenty minutes when Hassina came to a sudden halt. Freya and Jalay caught up with her a few seconds later. They stopped and stood astride their bikes. The path had come to an abrupt end. Ahead of them lay a deep gorge. The three girls stood together peering down into the chasm.

Freya couldn't contain her thoughts any longer. She began talking very rapidly and erratically. "Is there another way around? Because if there isn't I would just like to mention that I don't have any experience with rock climbing or abseiling and that basically I'm not very good with heights at all! In fact, I'm feeling a little dizzy just standing near the edge." Jalay and Hassina looked at Freya. The pace of her confession stunned them. They were unsure how they would be tackling this obstacle. However, they both agreed they would not be going around. Any detours in their journey would delay locating the children and they would under no circumstance compromise their rescue. It was essential they reached the children as soon as possible. Freya continued to emphasise that she could not climb down the chasm. If that were the plan, she would be remaining at the top of the gorge until they collected her on their return journey. She didn't want to be the cause of any delay in rescuing the children. Jalay informed her that they would all be staying together.

Freya was about to speak but Jalay showed her the hand. She was now looking directly at Jalay's palm which was level with her eyes and was ten centimetres from her nose. Freya stopped in mid-sentence, giving Jalay the opportunity to speak. She told Freya she had something to show her. Jalay took a sketchbook out of her backpack and began flicking through the pages. Stopping at one of the drawings, she ripped the picture out of the book. Jalay then laid the piece of paper down onto the edge of the gorge. Freya was amazed but couldn't quite believe what was happening in front of her eyes. She questioned if it was some sort of illusion. Jalay had lain down a painting of a zip wire and it had become real.

Forgetting her fear of heights, Freya stood near the edge of the gorge and leaning forward she touched the wire. It was amazing. This was no illusion the wire was real. Freya was now lost for words. Hassina broke the silence by volunteering to go first. This snapped Freya back into reality. Shaking her head, she asked Hassina if she was serious. Freya tried to reason with the girls and appeal to their common sense. She couldn't believe they were going to put themselves in so much danger. They would be relying upon a picture for goodness sake! Just because it was real didn't mean it was safe. The girls could see Freya was becoming very anxious. Jalay put her arm around Freya's shoulder and tried to allay her fears telling her that everything would be okay. Unfortunately, she was not convinced and began pacing up and down. Ignoring Freya's protests, Hassina put on the safety harness and clipped it onto the wire. Smiling reassuringly at Freya, she told her not to worry. Freya found it difficult to return a smile. Jalay handed Gym to Hassina who held him tightly under her arm. Moving to the edge of the gorge, she casually stepped into the air. Freya placed her hands over her eyes. She was unable to watch. Hassina hung onto the strap of the harness with her left hand. She wrapped her right hand around Gym's waist and held him close to her body. His little legs dangled in the air. They both moved at great speed zipping along the wire. Gym barked excitedly and Hassina was shouting "yahoo!" She sounded as if she was having a great time. Freya couldn't resist peeping through her fingers to see what was happening. It was a long way across and Hassina was only half way there. Freya worried that the strap would break causing Hassina and Gym to go hurtling towards the ground.

When they finally landed safely on the other side Freya and Jalay heaved a sigh of relief. They cheered and jumped up and down hugging each other. Hassina ran around in circles waving her arms in the air like an Olympic medal winner.

Now it was Freya's turn. After a lot of persuasion and encouragement, she decided to be brave. Taking a deep breath, she began talking to herself. "I have to think positive. I can do this." Hassina sent the harness back across the gorge as quickly as she could. Jalay then helped Freya into the straps and attached the safety clips to the wire. All she had to do was step off the edge. Freya began shaking out her arms and legs as if she was an athlete limbering up for a big race. Unfortunately, as she was about to step off she was seized with panic and was unable to go any further. Freya feared the strap would break and she certainly wasn't ready to die. Jalay insisted that it was safe. She explained to Freya that Hassina was much heavier and she had managed to get safely across. Freya was adamant she was not going and no amount of convincing was going to change her mind. Turning to Jalay she looked directly into her eyes and spoke slowly emphasising every word "I cannot do it." Jalay stood beside her and put her arm around Freya's shoulder. Suddenly she gave her a big shove. Freya stumbled forward and her feet slipped off the top of the cliff. Unfortunately, she had only travelled a meter along the wire when she came to a halt. Freya was screaming and her feet kicked furiously towards the edge of the mountain. She stretched her legs trying to put them onto solid ground. It was futile; she couldn't reach. Swinging from side to side in mid-air, Freya began shouting. She asked Jalay if she was crazy. Jalay held in her laughter and apologised. She gave Freya instructions on how to proceed. She would have to release the brake, which was just above her head. In her panic to grab hold of the safety strap, she must have pulled the brake. Freya protested that she couldn't let go with either hand. If she did, she would fall. Jalay finally persuaded her to hold onto the strap with one hand and pull the brake with the other. After several reluctant attempts, she finally released the brake. Freya began zipping along the wire screaming. Her heart was pounding so much she thought it would burst through her chest. Her ears had popped. She wasn't sure if it was the altitude or the screaming that was causing the peculiar echoing sensation. Freya had never flown in an aeroplane. Her friends at school had talked about the strange feeling in their ears when taking off and landing. She hoped her hearing would return to normal. Her hands were sweaty. She gave each a wipe on her jeans, being careful to hold onto the strap at all times. Looking down, she could see a fast running river below her which wound between the mountains and disappeared into the distance. There were tall trees as far as the eye could see and she had a wonderful smell of pine in her nostrils. It was a huge relief when she finally landed safely on the other side. Hassina helped her out of the harness and sent it back along the wire for Jalay.

When Jalay reached them, she put her arm around Freya's shoulders and apologised for frightening her. She was reluctant to accept the apology initially and shrugged Jalay's arm away. A few minutes later, Freya realised that being moody was not going to be helpful even though she was in the right. She began laughing at herself and the girls joined in.

They set off along the trail looking for clues and hoping they were going in the right direction. Freya wanted to know about Romain. She had many questions which the girls did their best to answer. They talked about his amazing powers and the beautiful cloud palace. They became so engrossed in their conversation. Before they knew it, they had made their way down the mountain. Freya looked up at the sky. It was dusk. The girls decided there wouldn't be much point in continuing since it would be dark soon. They decided to set up camp for the night and would continue their journey the following day, as soon as it was light.

Freya hadn't seen any camping equipment. She assumed they would be sleeping on the ground under the stars. She was so tired she honestly didn't care where she slept. Freya selected a patch of even ground, peeled her backpack from her shoulders and plonked herself down. Jalay walked over to the base of the mountain and put her backpack on the ground. Taking a piece of paper out of her paint book, she placed a picture on the rock surface. Freya was intrigued. She heaved herself up and walked over to Jalay. She watched as the picture of a tent became real.

It was amazing there was a door in the centre and windows either side. Jalay grinned at her and walked inside. Freya peeped cautiously around the door. The tent stretched right back into the rock. She expected the mountain to come crashing down at any second. She was reluctant to cross the threshold and chose to remain outside. Hassina brushed past Freya and entered the tent. She returned to the entrance a short time later and instructed Freya to get her backpack and come inside. Freya shook her head. She didn't think the structure looked safe. Hassina reminded Freya of the zip wire and told her that she needed to start trusting them. They had a long journey ahead and if she didn't have confidence in them, she would put all their lives at risk. Freya protested that she did trust them. Hassina held out her hand and asked Freya to prove it. Freya smiled; she took Hassina's hand and walked inside.

It was unbelievable. The roof of the tent was high enough to stand up right and walk around. There was no evidence of the mountain which pleased Freya immensely. Bright lights hung down from the ridge bar illuminating the contents of the tent. On the right side, there were three camp beds. Each bed had a sleeping bag and pillows. On the opposite side of the tent was the kitchen and dining area. The table was laid with plates, cutlery, and glasses. There were three wooden chairs at the table. It reminded Freya of the fairytale 'Goldilocks and the three bears'. She began laughing to herself. Hassina had switched on the oven and was preparing the evening meal. Freya walked over to the fridge and opened the door. Astoundingly, it was actually cold. When she looked inside there was a marvellous selection of fresh food on every shelf. It was amazing.

She couldn't contain her excitement and jumped up and down clapping her hands. Hassina and Jalay remained very calm and seemed to be taking things in their stride. Eager to get involved she asked what she could do to help. Jalay suggested she switched the kettle on and made a cup of tea for everyone. In no time at all the meal was ready and they sat down to eat at the table. They had prepared chicken, chips and corn on the cob. For pudding, there was hot chocolate fudge cake and fresh cream. They laughed and chatted about the day's events whilst they enjoyed their meal. Gym was included in the feasting. He was back to his large stature and his meal reflected this. He'd had a huge bowl of meat and as a special treat he was given a juicy bone which he took to his bed and began gnawing.

When they had finished their meal, Hassina suggested they settled down for the night. Gym slept on a blanket near the entrance of the tent. He would be their early warning signal in case of an intruder in the night.

Exhausted, they lay on their beds and continued to talk about the day's events. Freya told the girls it had been the strangest day of her life. She wondered what tomorrow lay in store for them. The girls assured her that things would probably become even more bizarre as their adventure progressed. It was nine o'clock and although it was only early, they all agreed it would be wise for them to settle down for the night. They would have a long day ahead of them tomorrow. They switched off the lights and snuggled down into their sleeping bags. They lay awake chatting for a while until one by one they finally drifted off to sleep.

The next morning Freya was awoken by the wonderful smell of cooked bacon. Opening her eyes, she stretched out her arms and yawned. Hassina and Jalay had been up and dressed for a long time. They thought it best to leave Freya to sleep for as long as possible. The girls had cooked a full English breakfast and hot buttered toast. Freya made a pot of tea and poured herself a glass of fresh orange. The four of them tucked in to a hearty breakfast. When they had finished eating, Freya showered in the bathroom at the rear of the tent.

They collected their belongings and the camp was packed away. Well that is to say, Jalay took the picture down from the mountain rock and neatly folded it. She then put the picture safely back into the sketchbook and put the book into the backpack. They were now ready to get started once again.

Freya was curious to know how far they would have to travel. Jalay was unsure. She suspected they would probably be walking a lot further than the previous day. Freya suggested that Jalay might like to paint a car or some other form of transport. This would enable them to find the missing children a great deal sooner. Jalay appreciated Freya's suggestion.

Unfortunately, she was going to have to disappoint her. Only pictures painted within the attic could become real. Jalay also reminded Freya that none of them could drive. Freya was a little disheartened. She didn't like the sound of the journey that lay ahead of them, particularly if they were walking. She asked if they could have the bikes back. Jalay was surprised. She thought Freya had experienced enough cycling the day before. However, if Freya would rather cycle than walk Jalay didn't have a problem with that. She pulled the picture book out of her backpack and tore out a painting. Laying the picture against the mountain their three bicycles appeared.

They rode through the forest and admired how magnificent it was. Everyone was amazed by the tall tropical trees and the huge green leaves which hung over the path. There were colourful flowers which lined the pathway. They released an aroma of perfumes which the girls inhaled as they peddled along. The birds had magnificent plumage the colours were so vibrant. The girls were enticed from their bicycles by the birds haunting hypnotic music. They danced around in a daydream oblivious of their surroundings.

Gym tried to break the spell by continually barking. This made no impact at all. Suddenly, something caught his attention further along the trail and he ran off in pursuit of it. Sometime later, he returned to find the girls were still lost in the music. Gym made one final attempt to get the girls attention. He nipped Hassina's hand with his sharp teeth causing it to bleed. Feeling an intense pain brought Hassina to her senses. Glancing at her watch, she realised that they had been listening to the birds for two hours. They needed to escape. However, no matter how hard she dragged, pushed, and pulled Jalay and Freya they remained mesmerised. They were flouncing around like fairies unaware of their performance. Hassina laughed to herself. If they could see how ridiculous they looked they would be mortified. Freya normally danced to music by her favourite band 'One Direction'. Jalay liked to listen to heavy metal bands such as 'Running Wild'.

Hassina could feel herself drawn to the bird's music once again. She knew she needed to act quickly. She promptly took her Ipod out of her pocket and put in her earplugs. Turning up the volume Barry Manilow's 'Copacabana' drowned out the bird's hypnotic tune. She took the picture book out of Jalay's backpack and ripping out a painting, she laid it on the ground. It was a picture of three sets of headphones. When the painting became real, she quickly picked up two sets. She placed a pair over Freya's ears and then Jalays.

They became aware of their surroundings almost immediately. Grasping hold of the girl's hands, Hassina led them towards their bicycles. She gestured to them to get on their bikes and ride as fast as they could. There was to be no stopping and no turning back. After riding for a good hour, Hassina decided to remove her earplugs. She was curious to know if they had escaped the clutches of the birds hypnotising melody. She could hear the rustle of rabbits hopping close by in fallen leaves. Thankfully, there was no music. They were safe at last. Everyone thanked Gym for his quick thinking. Hassina sat him in the basket at the front of her bicycle once again .The sun was shining, the sky was blue and they all felt wonderful. Freya couldn't help wondering 'If not for Gym, how long would the birds have kept them prisoner?' The thought of being hypnotised by the birds for two hours was frustrating and frightening. They had not realised how vulnerable they were. Despite their beautiful surroundings, they would all have to be more vigilant if they were going to survive in their pursuit of the children.

CHAPTER 5

VOICES

The girls cycled around the mountain until midday when Hassina suggested they stop for something to eat. Jalay then placed a picnic blanket on the ground. She produced lots of goodies from her backpack such as sandwiches, crisps, and cold drinks. They all sat down and began eating their lunch.

Hassina suddenly pointed to a particular section of the mountain. When the others looked up, they could see what appeared to be a cave. It was approximately half way up the mountainside. Hassina and Jalay were intrigued and very keen to explore. Freya, however, was not. She gave a sigh and a little groan at the thought of having to climb up the steep rocks. Unconvinced by the need to investigate the cave she questioned their purpose. She wondered if the journey was necessary. The girls reminded Freya that they must investigate at every opportunity no matter how remote the possibility of discovering the children.

The girls voted and out-numbered Freya two to one. They abandoned their bikes and all began their ascent. Freya was not as fit as she should have been for a young girl of her age.

She could dance for hours. However, walking and climbing were not at the top of her list of things to do. Consequently, the girls had to listen to Freya moaning and groaning as they scrambled up the mountainside. On reaching the ledge in front of the cave, Freya collapsed on her back out of breath. Dramatically, she demanded water in the same way a person would who had been lost in a desert for days. After having a cold drink, they encouraged Freya to get to her feet.

The girls then made their way across the uneven rocky ledge to the mouth of the cave. They stood at the entrance gazing in at the pitch-blackness. Hassina took a flashlight out of the backpack and switched it on. She entered the cave with little Gym, closely followed by Freya and Jalay.

Once inside Gym ran off into the darkness and disappeared. Freya was eager to look for him but Jalay told her not to worry. Gym was an independent little dog and was used to fending for himself. He would find them when he was ready.

Freya was uneasy in the cave. The hairs on her exposed arms stood on end and a shiver travelled down her spine. Undoing the jumper tied around her waist, she put it over her head and pushed her arms through the sleeves. Pulling the jumper down, she gave a shudder. Freya felt a little more protected now. It was like putting on a suit of armour.

Treading slowly and carefully, they walked further into the cave. Hassina led the way with her flashlight followed by Freya and then Jalay. The floor of the cave was extremely uneven. They all took turns in tripping up. Fortunately, they were able to stop each other from falling.

Jalay suggested it may be safer to walk at the side of the cave. This would enable them to use the wall as extra support. Placing one hand on the surface, they felt their way around the cave. Their hands became wet and cold very quickly from the water running down the walls. Freya pulled her hands inside the sleeves of her jumper and tried to warm her fingers. They continued to go deeper into the cave. Freya was feeling a little claustrophobic and was eager to turn back before they got lost. The girls wanted to press onwards and dismissed her request to give up.

Shining the torch around the cave, they could see there were a great number of passageways. It was difficult for the girls to decide which path to take. Hassina and Jalay started searching for clues. They were looking for anything that would indicate the children had passed through the cave. Poor Freya didn't know what she was searching for and she looked to the girls for guidance. They asked her to look for footprints. She found it impossible to see anything without a flashlight. With a big sigh, she started to examine the passageway floor.

In the distance, she could hear a child's voice. Jalay and Hassina were close by discussing which path to take when Freya shushed them. They did as she asked and the three of them stood in silence. The girls wondered what they were listening for. Freya was surprised they couldn't hear the child's voice. Jalay and Hassina could only hear the water dripping down the sides of the cave. The voice then disappeared.

Freya explained that she had heard a child's voice calling her name. Suddenly she was shushing Hassina and Jalay once again. The voice was back. Freya was determined to find the child and following the echoed sounds, she led the girls into one of the passageways. Once inside they discovered several clues on the floor. One of the children had cleverly dropped charms from a bracelet. It reminded Freya of the story of Hansel and Gretel. Whilst Hassina and Jalay examined the clues, Freya raced through the passageway. She could still hear the voice. She was convinced she was very close to discovering the children. The girls followed and asked Freya to slow down. She was going too far ahead and they were frightened she would get lost. Freya could hear her name being called very clearly by what sounded like a little boy. She knew he was close by. Hassina caught up with her and reassured her, the children were not there. Freya was unconvinced and tried to push past Hassina. Jalay then grabbed hold of Freya's arm reiterating that she was mistaken and the children were not in the cave. Freya became cross and tried to break free from Jalay's grasp. She was positive that the children were just up ahead and nothing they could say was going to change her mind. Freya couldn't understand why Hassina and Jalay were pretending not to hear the child calling out.

The girls explained that the voice was talking only to Freya's mind. The children were not there, it was just a telepathic echo. Having Freya's full attention, they went on to explain that she had obviously been exercising some of her mind speak powers. Freya didn't understand. She was just Freya who wasn't particularly good at anything never mind possessing telepathic powers. The girls promised her that this would be only one of many talents she would learn to develop in the future. Freya was disappointed that she hadn't found the children. However, her disappointment was short-lived. She immediately became intrigued by the mind speak revelation. In the past, there were many occasions when she had been able to sense when things were wrong and sometimes she had been able to predict that certain things would happen. Being able to communicate with a stranger's mind was awesome! Freya wondered if this had happened because she had gone through the painting and if so what other powers would she possess. This was mind-blowing information. Whilst she was thinking about her super powers, they came to the end of the passageway. Hassina then led them into a huge cavern. It had large stalactites hanging from the ceiling. They were different sizes and colours, each resembling precious stones. There were diamonds, rubies, emeralds, and onyx. Glistening and glowing in the dark. The girls looked in wonderment as Hassina shone the torch around the cave. Freya thought it was so cool. She looked up and turned around in circles amazed by this spectacular sight.

All at once, there was an overwhelming feeling that something awful was going to happen. A terrible feeling of fear crept into Freya's mind. From the darkness of the cave behind them came a strange, frightening noise. The ground began to rumble, gently at first and then it began to shake fiercely. The girls found it difficult to stay upright and clung to each other for balance. The stalactites began to tremble a little initially, then as the girls looked upward, they could see them vibrating fiercely. Fearing for their safety, they dashed to the edge of the cavern.

Fortunately, they were standing with their backs against the wall when a large red stalactite crashed to the floor, missing Freya by a few inches!

The girls heaved a sigh of relief and laughed nervously at their near escape. Their laughing was interrupted by a haunting groaning noise that filled the cavern. Freya looked at the girls with wide eyes. There was panic in her face. She wondered what could have made such a dreadful noise. Whatever it was, it did not sound friendly. Jalay told Freya to stay close. Hassina shone the torch around the cavern. As they looked deeply into the darkness, they could see several pairs of red-rimmed eyes looking back at them. The girls squinted and tried to make sense of what they were seeing. They heard growling and snarling from yellow teeth suspended in the blackness.

Freya sensed it was time to run. Jalay agreed she grabbed Freya's hand and they sprinted further into the cave. It was very dark and the ground was uneven. The difficult conditions made it impossible for them to find their way without stumbling. Hassina did her best to guide them with the torch. They ran through several narrow passageways closely pursued by the growling creatures.

The girls had just turned yet another corner when Hassina let out a shout. She had lost her footing. Freya and Jalay could only watch helplessly as Hassina and the torch plunged into a deep cavern. The light from the torch bounced its way down into the darkness and eventually disappeared. Freya and Jalay were now in complete darkness. They called Hassina's name and waited in silence. There was no response from the dark chasm. The only sound was the growling noises from the darkness behind them. Hassina was beyond their help for the moment. Realising it was futile to remain there and fearing the noises behind them, they reluctantly began running.

Hassina had fortunately rolled down the cavern on her back. On reaching, what she thought was the bottom; she stood up trying to get her bearings. Suddenly the floor gave way beneath her and she found herself sliding down a narrow steep muddy tunnel. The tunnel had lots of twists and turns. The further she travelled the faster she went. She could feel her arms being scratched and bashed by protruding rocks. Feeling it would be safer to be stream lined; Hassina folded her arms across her chest and tucked in her chin. This protected her elbows from further injury. Keeping her eyes open, she searched in the dark for any sign of light. She was unable to see anything.

Hassina came to the end of the muddy tunnel and suddenly she was catapulted under water. Fighting her way to the surface, she found herself in an underground river. The current was very strong and the fast flowing water was pulling her along. Hassina swam towards the edge of the river, grasping at the sides. If she could just manage to hold onto something, she may be able to pull herself up and climb out. The water swept her along at such a furious pace that she was unable to grasp anything. The undercurrent continually sucked her below the water line. Fortunately, she fought her way to the surface on each occasion.

Hassina could see daylight up ahead but her relief was short lived. There was a tremendous noise in the distance, which became louder as she approached the light. The river was now slightly elevated. Looking down she could see a waterfall. There was a tremendous drop. The river was flowing so fast she could see no way of stopping herself. She tried to grab onto the sides of the bank but it was too high and very slippery. On her approach to the waterfall, she could see a large rock sticking out of the water. The current swept her close to the rock and she made a grab for it. Unfortunately, the river flow was too strong. No sooner had she secured her hold, then her fingers began to slip and eventually the water pulled her away. That was her last hope. There was nothing else she could do to save herself. She would be going over the waterfall. Hassina thought she may be able to ride the water like a slide. However, as she began to go over, the sheer pressure of the water pushed her below the surface. For a split second, she lost her breath and then splash! She was in a deep pool. Panicking she swam upwards towards the light.

Hassina finally emerged coughing and spluttering. She now found herself in a blue lagoon. She had made it and was safe at last. Swimming towards the bank of the lagoon, her thoughts turned to Freya and Jalay. She hoped they had managed to escape from the cave.

Freya and Jalay were frantically running through the tunnels closely perused by growling creatures. The girls had no source of light. Miraculously, they had managed to avoid colliding with the walls of the cave. Freya wondered if they had acquired sonic powers like bats. Jalay hated to disappoint her. However, she did point out that they had probably become accustomed to the darkness.

They turned a corner and Freya took a split second to look over her shoulder at their pursuers. She could see the outline of a grey shadow. The teeth were not human and certainly didn't belong to any animal she had ever known. The noises the creatures made sent chills right through her body. Freya had never been so frightened but was so glad she wasn't alone. Jalay kept reassuring her that the exit was just up ahead and told her to keep running.

Freya was instructed to start climbing. Jalay had pointed upwards to a ledge, which ran along the top part of the cave. They had to scramble up a steep incline, which was very uneven and full of rocks and boulders. Climbing up to the ledge, Freya could hear the grey shadows scrambling behind them. The creatures were getting closer. They appeared more agile than Freya and Jalay. Their vision seemed accustomed to the dark surroundings.

When the girls reached the narrow ledge, they could see the day light glowing in the distance. Freya led the way as they raced towards it. Jalay snatched her backpack from her shoulder and pulled a piece of paper from the sketchbook. She hurriedly pushed the book into the backpack and hurled the bag forward. It whizzed past Freya's head and landed outside the cave. At that moment, a shadow creature grabbed hold of Jalay's jumper causing her to stumble. Both Jalay and the creature travelled forward through the air. With the picture in her hands and her arms out stretched, she fell against the mouth of the cave.

Freya, who was just inside the cave entrance, was pushed forward by the picture. She found herself flying through the air into the daylight. She landed on the floor outside the mouth of the cave. Scrambling to her feet, she looked behind her. She saw a thick metal portcullis sealing the cave entrance. Jalay was nowhere to be seen. Worried that she may be lying injured, Freya began searching the bushes near the cave entrance. It didn't take her long to realise that Jalay must still be in the cave!

Freya ran towards the metal gate. Grasping hold of the bars, she tried to push the gate open but had no success. She then attempted to lift the metal bars. Once again, she was unsuccessful. The gate was impossible to move. It was securely fixed to the mouth of the cave. Freya shook the bars and shouted Jalay's name but there was no response.

Freya had an idea. She knelt down and frantically riffled through her backpack. Finally, she located her mobile phone. She switched it on and shone the light through the bars. Waving the light around in the dark, she saw something moving.

Jalay was being held by a grey shadow on either side of her. Freya was horrified and called out to her. She wanted to help but she didn't know what to do. Jalay told Freya to run but she refused to go. One of the shadows struck Jalay. She let out a scream and fell to the floor. Freya was outraged and began shouting at the creature to stop.

Suddenly a grey shadow appeared on the opposite side of the gate. The creature lunged forward its arms stretched through the grill. Freya dropped the phone in terror and fell backwards. The gate shook as the creature hurled its body against it. Fortunately, it held fast. Freya was safe for now. As it leaned through the gate, she was able to get a good look at the enemy. The surface of the creature was transparent; it had thin fingers with long dirty talons. Its eyes were black with red circles around the rim. Sharp yellow teeth filled a very large mouth. The creature drooled foul smelling saliva, which made Freya feel sick.

Trembling and shaking, Freya sobbed. Picking up her phone and the two backpacks, she began wandering along the path down the hillside. Big Gym came bounding towards her barking and wagging his tail. She was so relieved to see a friendly face. She bent down and hugged him. They walked together and had only travelled a little way when Freya heard her name being called. It was Hassina. She couldn't see her but she was able to follow the sound of her familiar voice. At last Freya caught sight of her through the trees. They began waving and calling to each other. Freya and Gym climbed down the grassy slope and eventually arrived at the water's edge. Looking across to the far side of the lagoon, they could see Hassina sat on a rock.

Gym jumped straight into the water and began doggie paddling towards her. Unfortunately, it was impossible for Freya to swim across. She had two backpacks to carry. Freya knew how important it was to keep the picture book safe and dry. The sketches were vital to their success. Jalay had entrusted her with the backpack and she was going to protect it at all costs. She would have to climb over the rocks and boulders which lay around the edge of the lagoon. Freya wore her backpack and carried Jalay's bag above her head. Stepping from rock to rock, she was able to balance with her knees bent and her body crouched down low. Fortunately, the depth of the water at the edge was only waist level. She discovered this on a couple of occasions when she slipped off the rocks. Luckily, she was able to keep the paint book dry. Freya constantly turned her head to look behind her. She was expecting to see a shadow creature in hot pursuit. Her paranoia was the reason she had lost her footing and slipped into the water.

Half way around the lagoon Freya stopped to look across at Hassina. She smiled as she watched Gym shaking his wet coat all over her. Freya sighed. It was taking longer than she thought to reach the relative safety of the other side.

Finally, she stumbled into Hassina's arms. Burying her face into Hassina's shoulder, Freya wept uncontrollably. Hassina comforted her by stroking her hair gently and reassuring her that everything was going to be all right. When Freya tried to tell her about Jalay, she was gently told to hush. Hassina knew Jalay had been captured. The ladies had communicated with each other's minds just before she had been taken away. Freya started to compose herself. She lifted her head from Hassina's damp shoulder and wiped the tears away from her red swollen eyes.

Freya feared the shadow creatures would eat Jalay. Hassina laughed. However, seeing the despair in Freya's face she stopped abruptly. She reassured Freya that Jalay would be a very valuable prize to her captors. Who, incidentally, were vegetarians. Freya was relieved to hear this. Hassina explained that the shadows were not in control. They were mere puppets and a very powerful force was pulling their strings.

A little more reassured, Freya stood up from the rock she was sitting on and walked over to the water's edge. Gym joined her and he began drinking the water. Freya knelt down put her hands into the cool lagoon and splashed her face. Now refreshed, she was ready for anything. She paused to look at the waterfall and marvelled at how beautiful it was. She wished they had the time to swim in this amazing pool. It was Freya's idea of paradise.

Hassina's thoughts turned to Jalay. She was a very resourceful young woman who could cope with anything life had to throw at her. Unfortunately, Hassina was unable to contact her mind. Something was blocking their thoughts. The girls realised they would be forced to carry on without her.

Hassina hoped they would be able to free Jalay and the children very soon.

She called to Freya and told her they needed to get moving. It was imperative that the girls travelled as far as they could physically manage during the daylight hours. They had to create as much distance between them and the pursuing creatures as possible. The grey shadows liked the darkness, which meant they could travel very quickly at night. If they were going to avoid capture, they needed as much of a head start as possible. Hassina was surprised they had encountered the Gloamins. She thought they would have passed through the area some time ago.

Freya asked how long the bars would hold the creatures back. Hassina wasn't sure how much time they had. She felt the gate would ensure they had a good head start. Hoping the children have left more clues, Hassina was optimistic they would pick up their trail if they left immediately.

CHAPTER 6

MEMOIRS

MEANWHILE BACK IN THE FOREST

Hassina and Freya made their way through the forest in silence lost in their thoughts. They missed Jalay terribly and worried about her fate. They continued to search the ground for clues hoping to find more bracelet charms. Unfortunately, they couldn't find anything at all to help them track the children.

Freya broke the silence. She wanted to know more about the Gloamins. Hassina was keen to take their minds off Jalay's disappearance and was pleased to share her knowledge of the shadow creatures. The Ledremain people had existed since time began. They were a closed society who discouraged strangers.

The Gloamins arrived on Ledremain, one dark winter's night thirteen years ago. Apparently, their planet Ravistat could no longer sustain the Gloamin nation.

The Ledremain's felt obligated to help them. However, they initially treated the creatures with suspicion.

The Gloamins lived in caves in the out lands of Ledremain. An invisible protective shield separated the two nations. The shield was controlled by the minds of the senior elders and was to remain in place until a final decision was made. There were many heated discussions and debates within the council chambers. Not all of the citizens accepted the Gloamins presence. Some of the Ledremain dwellers objected strongly and protested on the streets. An interim decision was made. The Gloamins were allowed temporary residence. However, the Ledremain people were to be vigilant at all times.

In the beginning, the Gloamin community was isolated. They lived in caves and underground dwellings, preferring dark damp places; no one knew what effect the daylight had on the creatures. The Gloamins would work at night. As soon as the sun rose, they would disappear under ground once again. As time passed, the elders removed the protective barrier and the two races co- existed. There was harmony and trust between their nations. The Gloamins shared their knowledge of how to grow different types of foods underground. They would grow strange fruits and vegetables, which tasted delicious. They gave their produce willingly. The Ledremain people attended to the Gloamins sick with their amazing healing powers. The majority of Ledremains befriended a Gloamin family and the children from both communities played together.

The Gloamins occupied the night and the Ledremain citizens continued their normal lives in the daylight. It was a perfect arrangement.

Freya was surprised the Gloamins had possessed the technology to transport themselves to another civilisation. Hassina agreed. The senior elders suspected that at least one of the Ledremain council members had assisted them. Hassina's voice then became angry. She told Freya that Ledremain was then deceived. The people let down their guard and were unprepared for what happened that terrible night.

At midnight, the Ledremain citizens were woken by Gloamins entering their homes and were forced to flee for their lives. Those who didn't escape were rounded up and taken away. She then began to describe what had happened to their family.

Hassina and Jalay were sat in a wooden boat, in the garden, at the back of the house. They waited for the others. There was so much confusion in the streets, they could hear people screaming and shouting. In the distance, there were buildings on fire. At last, the others came out of the house and made their way towards them. Edmortar brought the eight-month-old baby from beneath his green hooded robe and carefully placed her into the arms of Jalay. He then began helping his wife Sapera into the boat. Suddenly a grey shadowed creature grabbed her from behind and the three of them tumbled onto the grass. Edmortar shouted to his son Sithe to cut the rope, which anchored the boat securely to the ground. Edmortar continued wrestling with the creature. Sithe took out his pocketknife. It was a birthday present from his grandfather and this would be his first opportunity to use it. After a short time and lots of grunting and groaning, he managed to cut through the rope.

The boat was now free and began to rise into the air. Sithe watched as it floated above his head. Hassina could hear his thoughts. He was sure his father would be pleased. He had done something he was asked to do straight away and successfully as well. He turned to speak to his father, but the smile on Sithe's face quickly faded. His father was wrestling with the shadow creature. Sithe adjusted his eyes to the darkness and found his mother lying motionless on the ground. Gently stroking her hand, he tried to rouse her. She did not respond and Sithe became increasingly distraught, shouting for his mother to wake up. His father was a large, strong man. He was very strict and very rarely showed any affection towards him. His mother was petite, gentle, and kind. She understood him. When he was upset, he would speak to her about his troubles. If anything happened to her, he would be devastated. Gaining no response Sithe resorted to shaking her.

Sapera gradually became more responsive and opened her eyes. She smiled and stroked his face. She was concerned to see so much fear in her young son's eyes. Edmortar finally managed to defeat the shadow creature. There was no mercy shown towards it. He had the creature pinned to the ground, his foot firmly on the Gloamins chest. He drew his Ketarian from the leather sheath which was tied around his waist. For a fraction of a second, it glistened in the moon light. The creature whimpered as it saw the sharp metal lowering. Sapera who was now on her feet pulled her son inside her cloak and held him tightly. She wanted to shield him from seeing the demise of the creature.

The rowing boat was quite high now. If the girls jumped to the ground they would hurt themselves, or they may injure the baby. Jalay heard her father's voice in her mind. "Take care of your sister and you girls take care of each other. We will be there when you land." As the girls drifted away, their three loved ones on the ground became smaller. Hassina took hold of the oars and began rowing through the silent sky. The skyline was now completely red. Thick smoke filled the air making it difficult for the girls to navigate. They tied their scarves over their nose and mouth and continued to row away from the danger. To protect the baby from the elements, Jalay placed the wriggling bundle under her cape. Whilst Hassina rowed, Jalay kept watch over the side of the boat and did her best to steer. Sapera, Edmortar and Sithe mounted their Similies.

A Similie was an animal created by the elders one year after a citizen was born. The animal remained with its Ledremain resemblance throughout their lives. Their faces had the characteristic features of their Ledremain companion so no one could mistakenly take the wrong similie. The body of the animal resembled a horse. The relationship between a Ledremain and a Similie was one of complete trust. They were a team and would always work together

Hassina heard Edmortar speak to Sapera's mind. He was annoyed that his son had not been in the boat when the rope was cut. He thought Sithe should be up there protecting his sisters. Sapera appealed to Edmortar not to be harsh with their son. Sithe had done as he was asked. Edmortar agreed. He patted his son on the back and they set off on their journey to pursue the girls.

Unexpectedly, the breeze dramatically increased and the air current forced the boat upwards. The girls had now risen so high that the cloud cover had become very dense. It was impossible to see anything below them. The land had completely disappeared. Hassina tried to row the boat downwards. It was hopeless; the wind was far too strong to fight against.

Hassina was thirsty so she stopped telling her story for a moment and took a mouthful of her drink. Freya was enthralled and urged her to continue. She wanted to know what had happened to everyone. Hassina didn't have all the answers but she was able to tell Freya about their rescue.

Exhausted, the three girls eventually fell asleep. Their flying boat drifted across the sky. Romain rescued the girls. He was concerned about their safety and made the decision to hide them in the attic. This was to be temporary until their parents could be located. He searched for survivors for many years. Unfortunately, he was unsuccessful. The Ledremain people had simply disappeared.

Romain had discovered three people in the boat that night: Hassina, Jalay and Jalay's baby sister. Freya took a sharp intake of breath. With trepidation, she enquired about the fate of the baby. She wanted to know the whole story no matter how dreadful the outcome. Hassina became very quiet. Freya was concerned and she prepared herself for devastating news. Hassina explained that baby Freya had survived. Freya stared in disbelief. She wasn't sure if she had heard correctly. Was she really the baby in the boat?

Hassina told Freya she was a Ledremain. The mother and father who had raised her were not her parents. They were guardians appointed by Romain to protect her and to watch for her powers developing. Freya then asked about Wesley. She was told he was not her brother but the son of her guardians.

Romain had decided not to put Freya in the attic. She was only a baby and had not yet developed any powers. She was in no imminent danger of being detected. However, as she had grown older, the grey shadows had begun to appear in the attic pictures. They had found her location. Someone had sensed her presence and guided the Gloamins there. That is why they had to take Freya with them. They couldn't have left her in the attic unprotected.

This information alarmed Freya greatly. She clasped her hands on top of her head. This revelation was so huge she couldn't believe it was true.

She didn't understand. If she was the baby in the boat, why had she continued to age but Jalay and Hassina had remained the same. She explained that when Romain had put the girls in the attic, he felt very guilty about shutting away two young people. He knew it was for their own safety but decided that they should not miss their childhood. So when they eventually had the opportunity to leave the attic, they became the same children who entered it all those years ago.

Freya and Hassina were cousins. Hassina had been staying with Jalay's parents. Her mother and father who were known as Sheria and Eladon had gone to a spiritual retreat for the weekend. She did not know what had happened to her parents. Unfortunately, Romain had been unable to locate them.

Tears of joy and sadness started to fall down Freya's cheeks. She was overwhelmed with information. It was difficult to accept that the life she had led so far was an illusion. She had found a sister and a cousin, which made her happy. Unfortunately, she had not only lost a brother and the parents she had known all of her life but also a brother and parent's she hadn't known. This made her feel very sad. She asked if Wes was aware of all of this. Hassina assured Freya that he wasn't. Freya could feel tears well up into her eyes. How would she tell him? They were so close. There was no time to dwell on her thoughts. Jalay desperately needed her help and she was going to make sure she got it.

Jalay had always wanted to be the one to tell Freya about her past. Hassina hoped she wouldn't be too disappointed. Freya gave her cousin a hug and told her not to worry. She was glad she knew her history. She didn't feel like an outsider any more.

Freya had many questions but there were two utmost in her mind. The first was, 'what was her real name?' She was curious to know if she had an alias like Hassina and Jalay. Hassina teased her by tapping her hands on the backpack. This was her impression of a drum roll. There was a long pause then Hassina announced that Freya's name was "Freya" tadah! Freya was a little disappointed. She was expecting an exotic name. Hassina explained that, on Ledremain, children were given their name one year after their birth. The naming ceremony was a very important celebration. It was also the day their Similies were presented to them. Jalay had decided Freya's name. She had chosen it from a Viking storybook. Freya was so proud and honoured to be named by her sister. She was relieved not to have to get used to being called anything other than Freya.

Her second question concerned her powers. Freya was curious to know what other special gifts she could expect to develop in the near future. Hassina told her that no one could predict when the gifts would be given or what the gifts would be. However, one thing was certain, they would be fabulous. With the pressing questions out of the way, Hassina decided it was time to get going and find Jalay and the children.

CHAPTER 7

LOAM

When they had stopped talking, Freya commented on how quiet the forest had suddenly become. Glancing around, they realised that the birds were not cheeping. A complete silence had fallen upon the forest. The girls had a strange feeling that something awful was about to happen.

Slowly they scrutinized the area and noticed a thin layer of mist rising up from the ground in the distance. The white haze then swirled towards them and gradually enveloped them. The girls were startled by the sound of twigs cracking; they tried to determine where the sound originated. However, it had now become increasingly difficult to see the surrounding forest as the mist developed into a thick fog.

Suddenly, they heard a loud noise in front of them. The girls looked around, their eyes wide with panic, but they couldn't see anything. Freya's first thought was Gloamins. She whispered her suspicion to her cousin. Hassina reassured Freya that the Gloamins would not risk being out in the daylight.

Gradually the fog dispersed into a thin haze and silence fell upon the forest once again. The girls held their breath. They heard a strange sound in the distance. Scanning the area they could see the ground up ahead had sunk inward and had formed two huge circular holes. The girls began retracing their steps. As they backed away they heard a similar sound behind them. They turned their heads, slowly and cautiously, not knowing what to expect. Another large circular void had appeared, preventing their exit.

They tried running to the right and then to the left but there was no means of escape. One by one, the holes appeared until, the girls were surrounded by huge circular hollows. Gym started barking and growling. The girls knew he was warning them of imminent danger. They held hands and braced themselves.

The mist gradually disappeared and revealed several large brown silhouettes. The shapes stood lifeless for a few seconds and then began climbing out of the holes. The girls could see large Loam beings made of chunks of soil which resembled body armour. Gym was barking and snapping at the brown shapes. He tried to frighten the huge creatures by increasing his size. He ran from one to the other, growling and snarling but with little effect. There didn't appear to be any possibility of getting past them and escaping. They were surrounded. One of

Mrs Jenkins favourite songs started playing in Freya's head, "Nowhere to run to baby nowhere to hide". Suddenly Gym spotted a gap and raced through it. He had managed to escape. Freya looked to Hassina for any ideas of how they were going to get out of this situation. Before they had the opportunity to discuss an escape plan, they were attacked!

The girls heard a high-pitched whistling sound above their heads .The air then became full of brown speckles. One of the Loams had hurled itself through the air by disintegrating its body into soil particles. The soil collided with its chosen target. In this instance, it was Hassina. The dirt wrapped itself firmly around her lower limbs and began squeezing. She was now unable to move. Another loose assembly of soil launched itself through the air. This time it landed on Freya's legs. The soil gripped hold of her. It was like a wrestler struggling to restrain its opponent. The girls could hear the whistling once again as the soil threw itself towards them. Unable to move, they put their hands over their faces and prepared themselves for an additional onslaught of earth. Their lower bodies were now enshrouded with living soil. Hassina and Freya began to sink slowly into the ground due to the sheer weight of the dirt clinging to them. Their knees had now sunk down to grass level. It was as if they were being sucked down by quick sand.

More and more soil converged in quick succession. The living earth crept up the girl's torsos and reached their shoulders within seconds. Freya couldn't see a way out and was shrieking at the soil to stop what it was doing.

Gym returned running around snarling and growling at the dirt. He placed his front paws on the mound of earth that surrounded Freya' s lower half and looked up at her. He was barking and had a distressed look in his eyes. Gym then began scratching at the soil and tried digging a hole. The soil fought back and sent him reeling. Undeterred he returned and began scrabbling away at the soil mound once again.

Freya was trying to stay calm. She hated having her movements restricted. She called to Hassina hoping she had had time to think of an escape plan. Hassina didn't answer her. Freya strained to turn her head and was horrified by what she saw. Hassina was not visible. She was completely covered in soil. Freya let out a huge cry "noooooooooo!" Her temper exploded. She had lost Jalay and she was not going to lose Hassina as well.

Freya felt something wrap firmly around her wrists. It was tugging her and was trying to release her from the grip of the soil. Her arms were pulled free from the dirt. When she looked up, she could see vines from a nearby tree had wrapped around each wrist. The pulling action of the vines was causing the soil to loosen around her legs and body. Unfortunately, no matter how hard she struggled, she was unable to break free. The pain in her wrists was becoming unbearable. Her arms became so stretched she was sure they would be pulled out of their sockets. The vines had almost won the tug of war. The soil now only possessed Freya's ankles. With one huge tug, she was finally free and found herself hanging by her wrists from the branches of the tree. Gradually she could feel the vines slip away from her wrists. Unluckily, this resulted in Freya plummeting to the ground where she landed with a thud.

Recovering almost immediately, she leapt to her feet. She ran towards the mound of soil that had engulfed Hassina. Freya was now screaming at the soil to release her cousin. She feared it was killing her. Grabbing handfuls of the dirt, she began digging the earth away from Hassina's face. Gym had now joined her and the pair of them attacked the mound of dirt. The soil was startled by their actions and loosened its grip. The earth then fell away from Hassina's body and started crawling along the ground.

The soil then re-formed into solid chunks once again. Although a little dazed and shaky on her feet, Hassina was able to stand with Freya's support. Hassina and Freya could hear the sound of earth moving once again. The girls stood back to back looking wearily around them. Two gigantic soil shapes appeared in front of them. Hassina and Freya took a defensive stance expecting another onslaught of soil action. They glanced at each other despairingly. The girls knew if the two mounds of dirt in front of them decided to hurl themselves in their direction, they wouldn't survive the assault. They would be buried alive. To the girl's relief, there was no further attack.

The smaller Loams stood in a line in front of the gigantic shapes. They were not the lively energetic Loams that had leapt on the girls earlier. They were very subdued and hung their heads. They resembled mischievous children whose bad behaviour had been discovered and were expecting to be sent to the naughty step. The two larger shapes were shouting at the smaller Loams. It appeared their actions had been part of a game. A very dangerous game, as far as the girls were concerned.

Hassina and Freya were brushing the soil out of their hair when the young Loams approached them. They stood in front of the girls with their heads still bowed. Hassina and Freya could only assume they wanted to say they were sorry. The adults stood behind their children and spoke in soil speak. It sounded like someone with a mouth full of food trying to gargle with mouthwash. However, the girls did get the impression they were being given an apology.

Hassina rummaged in her bag and began flicking through the sketchpad. She ripped out a painting and placed it on the ground. It was a picture of a huge ball. Hassina offered the ball to the soil children. They were very curious and it was obvious they didn't know what it was. Freya rolled the ball to the edge of the embankment and released it. The ball bounced off one tree and then hit another. The soil children excitedly began chasing after it.

Hassina and Freya took the opportunity to make their exit whilst the Loams were preoccupied. The girls ran away as fast as they could. They hadn't wanted to appear rude by leaving and not saying goodbye.

Unfortunately, they had wasted too much time playing in the dirt. Their priority had to be the rescue of Jalay and the children. The girls didn't stop running until the Loam shapes were completely out of sight. Freya and Hassina walked very briskly for several hours, only stopping for a few minutes at a time to rest.

When they arrived at the edge of the forest, the girls were overwhelmed by the spectacular view. The sun was setting on a lake, which gave the water a golden glow. Exhausted, they flopped down onto the golden sand and admired the magnificent sunset. Hassina eventually suggested they set up camp for the night. Although they desperately wanted to continue searching, they were simply too tired.

Hassina brought the tent painting out of the backpack and placed it against a large tree. Later that night, they lay on their beds in the tent. Reflecting on the day's events, Hassina praised Freya for her quick thinking regarding the tree vines. She had been pleasantly surprised by how quickly her cousin's powers were developing. Freya's ability to move the vines with her mind had been amazing. Freya was shocked she hadn't realised her mind had enabled the vines to rescue them. Laughing, she told Hassina she thought the tree had rescued them. Freya was very proud of her developing talents. Her actions had meant they were safe for another night. She was keen to talk about any other powers she might possess. Regrettably, Hassina was tired. She simply laughed and told Freya to go to sleep. They both settled down and drifted off very quickly whilst Gym kept watch over them.

CHAPTER 8

CAPTIVE

Two Gloamins dragged Jalay to her feet, one either side of her. The creature's thin bony hands grasped around her arms and their talons dug into her skin. Looking towards the daylight she could see one of the creatures was charging at the metal gate repeatedly. Fortunately, it held fast.

Jalay could hear sobbing in the distance. She thought of poor Freya, frightened and confused. At that moment, the Gloamins began dragging Jalay away. Freya's cries became fainter. Jalay was taken from the light and pushed deeper into the darkness of the cave. It was difficult to see where she was going as there was no torch to light her way. Only the strong arms of the Gloamins kept her from falling over. When she tripped, the talons of the creatures dug deeper into her flesh causing her to cry out in pain. They ignored her cries and continued to march further and further into the blackness. She tried to communicate with them and asked where they were taking her. Jalay's questions were ignored.

The labyrinth of tunnels merged into one. Many other Gloamins joined Jalay and her captors. The passageway now became extremely narrow forcing everyone to walk in single file. Jalay put her hands on the walls either side of her. She hoped this would stop her from falling over. She worried that if she did fall she would probably be trampled upon. Everyone was squashed together and Jalay was being carried along by the vast number of creatures.

The only source of light was a flame held torch. This was carried by a hooded figure at the front of the line. Continuing to follow the torch, they weaved their way through many passageways. Finally, they arrived at an underground waterway. Jalay could see there were many wooden ships lined up in rows. They were secured to the quayside by thick pieces of rope. Each vessel had a different grotesque figure head carved in wood at its helm. Walking past the ships, Jalay noticed the seating of each vessel didn't reflect the vast number of Gloamins in the caves. Jalay wondered if the creatures who were not travelling in the ships would be heading off in pursuit of Hassina and Freya.

Her Gloamin guards quickened up their pace and escorted Jalay to a ship near the front of the flotilla. There was now a great deal of pushing and shoving on the quayside. This escalated and some of the Gloamins began fighting. Two of the brawling creatures collided with Jalay and her escorts knocking them off the quayside and into one of the boats. As the three of them were launched through the air, Jalay screamed and prepared herself for a painful landing. She was surprised when she encountered something soft. Underneath Jalay and her two guards were several Gloamins, they had already been seated. They violently pushed Jalay and her escorts causing them to land on the floor in the middle of the ship. Her two guards grunted and snarled at the Gloamins around them.

When they were finally seated, one of Jalay's escorts grabbed hold of her hands and tied them together with a vine. Its face was now level with her. She watched as saliva slobbered down the creatures chin. This made her feel a little nauseous but she was unable to turn away. She was drawn to the creature's black eyes. Staring into them deeply, she saw no compassion, only emptiness. It appeared to be like a zombie. She suspected its movements were being controlled. The Gloamins either side of her grabbed an oar.

Freya was startled by the sound of a horn. She looked to the quayside and watched as the ropes securing the ships to the ring moorings were untied. The creatures took up their oars and placing them in the water, they began rowing. The vessels started to move away slowly from the quayside. The sound of the horn intensified the violence between the Gloamins who were trying to board the last few ships. A great number of them fell into the river. Jalay could see Gloamins lying face down in the water. The bodies floated past the boats, carried by the river current. Stood at the head of each of the boats were silver robed hooded figures. Jalay couldn't determine whether they were men or women. They didn't turn around throughout the whole of the commotion but kept their gaze fixed straight ahead. Jalay suspected the cloaked figures were exercising a form of mind control over the Gloamins.

After rowing for some time, they finally emerged from the cave. Jalay thought it was wonderful to breathe fresh air once again. The horrible damp earthy smell that had been overwhelming in the cave was no longer in her nostrils. Fortunately, it was dusk so her eyes were able to adjust relatively quickly from the darkness to the evening light. Looking around, Jalay couldn't get her bearings. She didn't recognise any of the landmarks from her paintings. There were tall black mountains ahead of them and thick forests on both sides of the river. They travelled through the night. The moon and stars were their only source of light. The boat followed the course of the river and travelled around many bends, weaving its way through the tall black mountains.

The sound of the oars splashing in the water became hypnotic. Jalay was tired. She sat in the bottom of the boat. Folding her arms on the seat she rested her head on her hands and drifted off to sleep. It was still dark when Jalay was disturbed by a loud shouting noise. Half asleep, she hauled herself to a sitting position and looked around to see what the commotion was. Most of the Gloamins were leaning against the side of the boat looking down at the water. Jalay stood on the wooden seat. She could see several large rocks sticking up from the riverbed. She suspected the ships would be unable to pass these obstacles.

Aware that the silver robes and her captors were preoccupied, Jalay seized the opportunity to try to communicate with Hassina. She sat down and concentrated. Unfortunately, her thoughts were blocked. There was a thick barrier in her mind. This frustrated her terribly. Jalay knew the girls would be worried about her. She just wanted to let them know she was okay. All of the ships had now stopped rowing. The oars were taken out of the water and were stood on end. The river current pushed their ship a little further until it finally halted. As Jalay looked around, all she could see was trees and mountains.

Her two captors pulled her to a standing position. She presumed it was time to disembark. Dragged down from the boat, she found herself waist high in water. It was difficult to balance with her hands tied but eventually she managed to steady herself. She waded through the stream towards the embankment. When she reached the rocky sand bank, she began to stumble. The two creatures became impatient and dragged her over the rocks. Her captors forced her to sit on the grassy embankment.

Jalay watched as all the ships were abandoned and the Gloamins poured from the river. When the creatures from the first three ships had arrived on shore, Jalay was hauled to her feet. She was forced to join the long line of creatures as they headed inland. She was wet, cold, and hungry but there was to be no rest. She stumbled and fell several times. Her hands were tied and she found it difficult to get up from the ground. She tried to communicate this to her captors but they simply ignored her and repeatedly jerked her to her feet. When they finally stopped to rest it was several hours later. Exhausted, she put her head against a tree and fell asleep. It seemed no time at all when Jalay was being forced to her feet once again. They continued to walk for hours through the darkness. Jalay was beginning to wonder how much longer she could continue without water.

Suddenly the procession came to a halt. Below them was a valley with a large encampment which was surrounded by high wooden fences. Beyond the camp was a rock face with numerous caves carved into it. The caves seemed to house hundreds of Gloamins. Dawn was breaking and the creatures suddenly became agitated. There now appeared to be a great urgency for them to get down to the encampment. A huge number of Gloamins covered the hillside. It was like a moving grey carpet.

The steep slope was slippery under foot. Jalay concentrated on trying to stop herself from falling over. Some of the Gloamins also had difficulty keeping upright. Several of them tumbled past her. She watched as they became impaled on the jagged boulders at the foot of the hill. She was relieved when she arrived at the bottom of the slope in one piece. Walking towards the enclosure she hoped she had reached the end of her journey. She was forced to halt in front of the high wooden gates. Her Gloamin escort grabbed hold of her wrists and pulled them up towards its mouth. The creature then sank its teeth into the vines and gnawed through them freeing her hands. The gate opened and Jalay was flung into the enclosure. The large wooden gate was then swiftly closed behind her. Wearily, she scanned the camp. A small boy with deep green eyes and blonde hair approached her. The boy introduced himself as Lyoneth. She looked down at him and saw a shackle around his ankle. This was secured to a large wooden pole in the middle of the compound by a lengthy chain. The boy looked up at her and smiled. He slipped his hand into hers and led her over to the other children who were sat on the ground. Jalay was invited to join them. One of the older children gave her a flask, which contained water. Jalay took a mouthful. She didn't think water could taste so good. She expressed her thanks.

The little boy, who'd introduced himself as Lyoneth, was very disappointed not to see Freya and wanted to know where she was. Jalay realised this must be the mysterious voice who had called to Freya in the caves. Jalay explained that Freya and Hassina would be there shortly to rescue them. She praised Lyoneth on using his mind speak to guide them to him. Jalay asked who had been clever enough to drop the charms from their bracelet. A blonde haired girl with piercing green eyes called Melie stepped forward. She was thrilled to accept Jalay's praise. Jalay reassured the children that Hassina and Freya would rescue them and get them all home safely.

The very young children gathered around her and she gave them all a reassuring hug. Lyoneth never let go of her hand. He was the youngest child and had obviously been very frightened by the presence of the creatures.

The older children updated Jalay on the camp activities. There was no sign of the Gloamins throughout the daylight hours. They could however be seen in the entrance of the caves. The children were left alone during the day. The Gloamins came out of their caves at dusk. The creatures would enter the compound and provide the children with their daily meal. They would then disappear back to the caves leaving a small guard patrolling the fence perimeter. Jalay wondered why the younger children were shackled. One of the older children told Jalay that when they had first arrived they had all attempted to escape. Unfortunately, they were recaptured. Knowing the older children would not leave the younger children behind, the Gloamins chained them up.

Jalay was curious to know how they had all come to be in the enclosure. Lyoneth pulled at her hand and she asked if he would like to tell his story first. He nodded and began to tell his tale about the night the world of Daluce was attacked.

DALUCE- a few weeks previously

Lyoneth jumped up out of bed. He had been woken by screaming which appeared to be coming from the street. He peered through the window but could not see anything. He was beginning to think he must have been dreaming. Suddenly his bedroom door opened and he saw his father was standing in the doorway. Lyoneth was instructed to get dressed quickly and to make his way down to the kitchen as soon as possible. He tried to question his father but was curtly told there was no time for questions. Lyoneth did as he was asked.

He arrived in the kitchen to find his mother, father and older brother. They were dressed in their long pale blue coats. His brother was assisting his mother. They were packing the leather travelling bag. Her voice was shaking as she gave him instructions. Lyoneth could hear his mother and fathers conversation in his head. His parents usually blocked him from their thoughts. Particularly when there was something important they didn't want him to hear. This time they had forgotten and something terrible was happening. His Father was talking about fleeing from Daluce. The boats in the forest were waiting to take them away. Lyoneth felt his parent's eyes upon him. They realised he was listening and blocked him out abruptly.

Lyoneth's mother spoke to him and told him they were all going on a journey. His mother asked him to be very quiet and reminded him that he mustn't ask questions or question anything he was asked to do. She knelt down and helped him put on his coat. It was pale blue with double-breasted silver buttons and a hood. He was six now and could fasten the buttons himself but his mother seemed to be in a hurry. He stared at her face and thought how beautiful she was and how much he loved her. She smiled at him and kissed him on the cheek. He wrapped his arms around her neck and hugged her. Rising to her feet, she turned to her husband who nodded his head. Lyoneth felt his hair being ruffled. When he looked up, he saw his brother smiling down at him. Before he could return a smile, his brother had turned away.

Their Father abruptly asked if they were ready to leave. They all nodded. Pulling up their hoods, they walked to a door at the rear of the house. His mother reached for his hand and held it tightly. Their Father opened the back door cautiously. Checking the coast was clear, they slipped into the dimly lit alley. People were running in different directions. There was fear in their eyes. Lyoneth could hear screaming in the distance and there was a strong smell of smoke in the air. When they looked to the horizon, they could see there were buildings on fire. His mother pulled him close to her and held his hand very tightly.

His Father led the way whilst Lyoneth, his mother and his brother followed. They walked briskly down the alley. Lyoneth found his father's pace was very fast and he had to run beside his mother to keep up. His father gave fleeting looks over his shoulder. Lyoneth wondered what his father was looking for but he knew better than to start asking questions. They made their way out of the alley and into the brightly lit street. It was crowded with people fleeing from their homes. Some had carts loaded with belongings. Others simply strapped their possessions to their backs. Lyoneth's mother gave her husband a nervous glance. She feared, with all this activity, they may become separated. His father's large stature and forceful manner carved a path through the crowds.

As they made their way through the next few streets, the area became more deserted. Walking passed the houses they could see that people had left in a great hurry. Their front doors were open and property strewn across the street. A cold wind blew and an eerie silence lingered in the air. Shadows appeared and then disappeared behind the rooftops.

Turning a corner, Lyoneth could see the forest was ahead of them. They halted. A discussion followed and it was decided that the men would remain behind. Lyoneth and his mother were sent on ahead to hide in the forest by the lake. His father and brother would join them later when it was safe. His mother leant down and held Lyoneth's face in her hands. She told him they needed to run as fast as they possibly could and mustn't stop for anything. She smiled and kissed his forehead. They held hands and sprinted towards the forest. Lyoneth tried to keep up. He was running as fast as he could. He looked up at his mother waiting for her to say everything was going to be all right but she didn't. She just kept looking ahead. Her hand was still gripped so tightly around his it was beginning to hurt.

Lyoneth looked back and could see his father and brother had been joined by several other blue-coated men. They were each holding a ketarian in their hands. Their silver weapons glistened in the moonlight. They were preparing to fight. His Father and brother had always sharpened their ketarians every evening. Lyoneth had questioned why they did this. He was told that they should always be prepared to defend themselves against night visitors.

They were a few feet away from the forest when suddenly his mother let out a gasp. Three grey shadowed figures stood in front of them. She pushed her son behind her. He immediately wrapped his arms around her hips and cautiously peeped around her waist. The shadows stepped aside, revealing a hooded figure in a long silver robe. The ominous stranger stepped forward. Lyoneth heard the silver robed figure call his mother by name .The voice obviously belonged to a man because of the deep, harsh, gravel like tone. The stranger then asked her if she knew why he was there. She gave no response. He then directed his gaze at Lyoneth and spoke to him. The man smiled menacingly and informed Lyoneth that he was an old friend of his mothers. The stranger then accused her of possessing his property. If it wasn't returned, he was prepared to hurt many people.

Lyoneth was furious that this outsider threatened his mother. This was not the conduct of a good man. In Daluce women were revered. He regarded this man's actions as cowardly.

Lyoneth's mother refused to be bullied. She would not give in to the menacing stranger. Lyoneth recognised his mother was angry; her mood changing hair had turned red. The stranger was now growing impatient. He recognised her defiance and realised she was not going to cooperate. He stepped forward and placed his hands on either side of her head. The stranger pressed his fingers into her beautiful angry hair. He whispered a rhyming chant and she was soon induced into a trance.

Lyoneth had observed mind manipulation before. The elders would train the younger men in mind control. However, this was much more powerful. This was a deliberate act to hurt his mother. She fell to her knees. Clutching her head, she tried to block Lyoneth out so he wouldn't feel her pain. The surge of energy was so intense she was powerless to defend herself. She had to protect her son.

The silver robe began to draw out the information from her mind. Lyoneth ran towards the cloaked silhouette. He had a notion that if he disturbed the man's concentration, his mothers mind would be able to break free. However, the tormentor simply raised his hand and swished it in Lyoneth's direction. He was lifted up into the air and hurled backwards, eventually landing face down in the dirt. Raising his head, Lyoneth could see his mother was now lying motionless on the ground. Kneeling beside her was a grey shadow creature. The shadow was rummaging through her leather bag. It was taking things out of the bag examining each item and then discarding them over its shoulder.

A few seconds later the creature leapt up from the ground, holding a small wooden box above its head. The box was about thirty centimetres long and twenty centimetres wide. The lid was dome shaped. A gold decorated key with a green sparkling stone was secured to the lid. Lyoneth was shocked. He had never seen the object before. He wondered what could possibly be in there to justify so much destruction and devastation. The creature handed the box to the silver hooded man. He lifted the lid and looked inside. An amazing glowing light engulfed him. He then snapped the lid shut and the light instantaneously disappeared. Clutching the box under his arm, he laughed and as he walked away, he instructed the creatures to bring the child.

Lyoneth had managed to crawl to his mother's side. He was trying to rouse her. Before he could wake her, two of the creatures snatched Lyoneth up from the floor. He struggled to get away. Trying to escape was futile. The more he wriggled, the deeper their talons dug into his arms. Lyoneth began crying. He was becoming hysterical. Suddenly he stopped.

The reassuring sound of his mother's voice was in his head telling him not to be frightened. Lyoneth's mother promised that they would find him and bring him home. He wasn't to worry if he couldn't hear her thoughts anymore. She stressed that he must not use his mind speak when the man in the silver robe was near. The man was very dangerous. Lyoneth was relieved that his mother was awake and was recovering from her ordeal. He desperately wanted to be with her. He knew she would find him and bring him home. She'd promised. The creatures dragged him away and that was the last time he saw his mother.

Jalay gave Lyoneth a big hug and told him how brave he'd been. She then listened to the other children's tales until darkness descended.

When night fell, the creatures entered the compound to deliver the evening meal. This disturbed the children particularly the younger ones. They cowered behind Jalay. The food provided wasn't very appetising. It was, however, hot and there was a lot of it. There was also fresh water for each of them. Jalay was sure that if left to the Gloamins, they would probably starve. She felt the silver robes were behind the hospitality. The Gloamins didn't remain in the enclosure. As soon as the food was served, the gate was locked. Although they couldn't physically be seen, they knew the creatures were there. They could hear them shuffling around the perimeter.

After they had eaten, the younger children settled down to sleep close to the campfire. Jalay and some of the older children sat and talked. She was eager to know how many silver robes had been seen since they had arrived at the camp. She sensed a powerful presence. Rescuing the children would not be easy. They discussed their escape plans until they finally fell asleep.

CHAPTER NINE

SPIKE RUSH

The following morning Freya and Hassina woke very early. They stood at the water's edge watching the sunrise. There were mountains on three sides of the lake. It appeared the only option available to them was to travel straight across the water.

Freya was quick to point out that she was a slow swimmer. However, she felt confident enough to swim the whole distance. Her main concern was what could possibly be lurking underneath the water!

Freya stood, pondering that thought, whilst Hassina walked back into the tent. When she returned, she brought the backpack with her. She took out a picture from Jalay's art book and lay it down at the edge of the water. The painting became real. Sitting in the water, was a large silver dinghy. Amazingly, it had a black out board motor. Freya felt this was just the coolest thing she had ever seen. She was very relieved that they were not going to be swimming across the lake. The girls would be having a leisurely boat ride and taking things easy. Freya was looking forward to spending part of their day on the water.

She was convinced that their journey across the lake would be over in no time at all. Hassina was a little more sceptical. She pointed out that the length of the lake was further than it looked and it would take them the best part of the day to get to the other side. Freya was surprised but bowed to Hassina's wisdom. She wasn't bothered as long as she wasn't walking, cycling, or climbing.

After breakfast, they packed away the camp and made their way down to the shoreline. Freya waded into the water and held the boat steady whilst Hassina lifted little Gym into the dinghy. Hassina then climbed in but as she did so, she stumbled. Fortunately, she managed to steady herself. Freya then scrambled aboard a little clumsily. She sat at the front with Gym. Hassina had decided to steer and operate the motor. She pulled the cord on the engine but it didn't start the first or second time. It was third time lucky and they were on their way.

It felt good to get out of the woods and to have the wind blowing through their hair. There was a warm breeze and it brought colour to their cheeks. Freya's fingers felt cool as she dragged her hands through the water.

They had been travelling for two hours when the engine began clunking and then suddenly stopped. Hassina tried to restart it.

She pulled on the cord several times but nothing happened. Freya jokingly asked if there was an oars painting in Jalay's picture book; Hassina shook her head.

They decided to pull up the engine and inspect the propeller. When they examined it, the girls agreed there didn't seem to be anything wrong. The blades were intact and there didn't appear to be anything tangled around them. They were mystified. The engine was lowered back into the water. Hassina began pulling the cord once again. It still wasn't working.

Freya looked across the lake and noticed the water had turned black and was very still. Something was wrong. She heard a scream behind her. She turned around just in time to see Hassina go crashing into the water. She suspected Hassina had lost her footing. Freya rushed to the side of the dinghy, expecting to see her cousin cursing and moaning. There was no sign of her. Freya became concerned. She worried that Hassina might have bumped her head on the side of the dinghy as she entered the water and knocked herself out.

Freya took off her sweater and shoes as quickly as possible. She was ready to jump in. She had passed her life saving certificate and felt sure she could put into practice what she had learnt.

Suddenly something grabbed her from behind. She fell back into the boat, smashing her head on the outboard motor. Freya let out a shriek! Despite the terrible pain in her head and feeling a little dazed, she managed to get to her feet. She grabbed the straps of the backpack and scanned the craft. She was relieved to see that whatever had grabbed hold of her was no longer in the dinghy. It was then she noticed that Gym was missing.

To protect herself, Freya used the backpack as a weapon and began swinging it around her head. The bag came into contact with something solid. She turned sharply, but the object had already entered the water. She had no idea what it was. As long as it wasn't in the dinghy, she didn't care.

She scanned the water; there wasn't a ripple to be seen. She was puzzled. If the lake was so still, why was the dinghy rocking from side to side. The swaying increased until the boat was shaking uncontrollably. Freya found it difficult to keep her balance. She sat down and clung to the rope which ran around the inside of the craft.

Out of the corner of her eye, she noticed something moving. Freya looked closely and could see eelgrass hands, creeping over the edge of the dinghy. Several heads then appeared. They were covered in a variety of brown and green fauna. This gave them a moist slimy appearance. Their round, black soulless eyes stared at her.

Freya was frightened but found it impossible to scream. Fear had gripped her throat. Her heart was pounding in her ears and she began to panic. The eelgrass lake monsters would be in the boat in a matter of seconds. She watched as the thin willow like figures began hauling themselves into the dinghy. Once onboard, the slimy monsters began crawling towards her. Suddenly she found her voice and began shouting at them. "What do you want, why are you here?" She screamed hysterically. "Get off my dinghy!" The lake monsters didn't answer; they merely fixed their gaze upon her and crawled towards her. Shuffling herself backwards, she perched herself on the edge of the dinghy. There was nowhere else to go now. If she moved any further back, she would fall into the water. At that moment, one of the monsters lunged at her. She quickly dropped the backpack in the dinghy. Freya and the monster toppled into the freezing cold lake. As she hit the water, pain began shooting through her head. She was unsure if it was a result of her previous head injury or the severe coldness of the water. When she opened her eyes, she found herself face to face with an eelgrass. Its slimy hands were deliberately applying pressure to her throat. Freya tried to release its grasp by pulling at its fingers. They felt squidgy as she tugged at them. Oddly, the grip around her throat remained firm. It was impossible to escape from its clutches. The monster started to force her towards the bottom of the lake.

Freya could see poor Hassina wrestling with another eelgrass figure. Her cousin was being pushed deeper into the blackness. She had slimy fingers wrapped around her arms, tightly gripping her skin. Hassina had been under the water for a long time and could feel the air being squeezed out of her lungs. She continued to struggle but was becoming weaker. She had now reached the bottom of the lake. Hassina and one of the lake monsters were rolling around in a forest of fauna. As they fought, her clothes were impaled on the spike rush. She was unable to move. She was beginning to lose consciousness.

Freya could hear high-pitched squealing sounds all around her. Suddenly, jolted sharply to the right, she found herself sinking towards the lakebed. Something had caused the lake monster to release her. Looking up she was amazed to see a fierce battle taking place between the eel grass monsters and a group of sea creatures she had never seen before. They had the head and dorsal fin of a dolphin but the body of a mermaid.

As the fight intensified, she saw the dolph-maids swim away in a large circular motion and then return at tremendous speed. Aiming their noses directly at their targets, they collided with the centre of the eelgrass torsos. Freya could then hear the water monsters groan and moan. They were knocked down into the spike rush and disappeared into the thicket of the fauna.

Having dispensed of the opposition, two of the dolph-maids swept down to the lakebed and gathered up Hassina on their noses. They held her gently and carried her to the surface. Freya laid alongside a dolph-maid. She held onto its fin whilst her rescuer wrapped an arm around her waist. They soared into the air, leaping over the dingy. Freya lost her grip and started to fall. She prepared herself to be immersed in the cold water for a second time. She was pleasantly surprised to find herself deposited safely in the dinghy. She was relieved to see a sopping wet Gym. He was busy shaking the moisture out of his coat. Exhausted, she managed to muster up the strength to grasp Hassina's wrists. With the help of Freya and Gym pulling and the two dolph-maids pushing, they managed to drag her into the dinghy. She was finally safe.

Freya laid Hassina down. Although wet, bruised and scratched, she was alive. She was in a fragile state and needed warmth and rest. Freya tried to make her cousin as comfortable as possible. She took a blanket and towel from the backpack. She wrapped them around Hassina's body and placed the backpack under her head. Hassina briefly opened her eyes. Freya smiled and encouraged her to rest. Exhausted, Hassina closed her eyes and fell asleep.

Reassured that her cousin was comfortable, her attention was drawn to a familiar high-pitched squeaky sound. She knelt at the side of the craft. Looking down at the water, she could see smiling grey faces. Stretching out her hand, she stroked the nose and head of the dolph-maid closest to her. It felt surprisingly warm. The dolph-maids then disappeared under the water.

She sat down beside her cousin and watched over her while she slept. It was an hour later when Freya noticed Hassina's eyelids flicker. Her eyes opened slowly and she smiled. The girls sat up with their backs against the side of the craft and huddled together under the blanket. Freya was telling Hassina all about their rescue from the deep when she heard the dolph-maids once again.

Freya opened the backpack and pulled out the sketchbook. After flicking through the pages, she ripped out a picture and placed it on the bottom of the dinghy. It was a painting of an assortment of dead fish. The girls picked up the fish and began throwing them into the water. The dolph-maids were ecstatic. They returned the girl's kindness by putting on an amazing display. They would disappear under water then reappear in the air performing all sorts of acrobatics. They were able to execute summersaults, individually at first, then in pairs and finally all six together. They arched their backs gracefully as they leapt over the dinghy. Hassina and Freya sat cheering and clapping at the incredible sight.

The dolph-maids disappeared beneath the surface of the lake once again but didn't reappear. The girls leant over the side of the dinghy searching for them. Disappointed, they sat back down hoping they would soon get another glimpse of their newly acquired friends.

The gentle warm breeze became cool and started to whip around them quite fiercely. When they looked upwards, the white clouds had blown away and were replaced by a grey sky. They could hear thunder in the distance and they knew a storm was heading their way.

Hassina flicked through the sketchbook and pulled out a picture. She placed the painting on the bottom of the dinghy. Two yellow rain coats and hats appeared. Freya declined to put her waterproofs on. Hassina reassured her that nobody would see her wearing the outfit. Freya decided she would rather get wet. Suddenly torrential sheets of rain began pouring onto the girls. Forced to abandon her fashion principles, Freya slipped the waterproofs on.

Sharp forks of lightening electrified the horizon. Gradually moving across the lake, it prodded the water as it crept along its surface. The lightning strikes created huge waves which washed over the dinghy, causing it to rock uncontrollably. The girls became more alarmed as the storm escalated.

Then, all of a sudden, it stopped. It was as if someone had flicked a switch. The lake became tranquil. The sky returned to a powder blue colour and the warm breeze wafted around them. The girls held their breath; they couldn't believe it. They had prepared themselves for the worst possible catastrophe. It seemed they were reprieved. Very soon, they would be safely on dry land. The girls could see their island destination in front of them. The distance to the shore was too far to swim. However, if they could get the engine started, they would reach the island in no time at all. Hassina made her way to the back of the dinghy and tried pulling the cord. To her amazement, it worked. The engine started first time.

The girls stood facing each other. Freya clapped and cheered Hassina's achievement. This would mean they could be on their way and escape from the lake. Hassina bent down and graciously took a bow to her appreciative audience. Looking beyond Hassina, Freya had a clear view of the horizon. She strained to see what looked like a blue wall with a white top. Hassina stood upright from her bowing position; she noticed her cousin was not smiling anymore. She asked Freya what was the matter. Freya simply raised her arm and pointed. Looking a little bemused, Hassina turned and looked behind her. The girls were horrified. Coming towards them was a wave that was at least fifty meters high. Freya put her fingers through her hair and grasped hold of the top of her head. She asked Hassina what they were going to do. Hassina thought for a moment and decided it would be a good idea to out run the wave.

Unfortunately, they soon realised the wave was travelling much faster than they could possibly go. They both agreed 'plan A' was not going to work. They needed a 'plan B'. Hassina came up with the idea that the only way to survive this was to ride the wave using the dinghy as a surfboard. Freya wasn't keen on the plan but since she didn't have an alternative suggestion. She was willing to go along with her cousin's idea.

Hassina kept the engine running and steered the dinghy to face the shore. Meanwhile, Freya sat in the front. She wrapped the rope around her wrist and then gripped it tightly. Her other hand held onto Gym's collar. The girls only had a few seconds to wait before the wave caught up with them. The powerful wave hit the back of the dinghy, sending the craft up into the air. Amazingly, the dinghy landed right side up. They now rode the length of the wave just below the white spray. Unfortunately, they were tilted to one side. The girls feared they would fall out. Hassina wrestled with the steering bar. She managed to keep pace with the wave and surfed the boat up and down. The wave continued to travel towards the shoreline at a tremendous pace. They prepared themselves for a crash landing. Everyone moved to the back of the craft. Lying low down in the bottom of the dingy, they pushed their limbs against the sides and braced themselves for impact. Suddenly, to the girl's surprise, the dingy came to an abrupt halt. The wave had stopped moving forward, enabling the dinghy to surf up to the top of the white crest. The craft now rested on the very top of the wave. Freya bravely peeped over the side and could see the white foam beneath them. The wave wasn't rolling forward, it had stopped in mid air about five hundred meters from the shoreline. Disastrously, the dinghy's engine stalled once again. Hassina frantically pulled on the cord but she couldn't get the engine started.

Gym wriggled free from Freya's grasp. He charged forward and put his paws up onto the front of the dinghy. The girls called to him to make his way back to them. Gym cautiously crawled back. It was too late. The craft started to teeter. The front end of the dinghy tipped downwards. It then slipped forward and began sliding down the wave towards the shore at a terrific speed. The force of the plunge caused Gym and the girls to become wedged into the back of the dinghy. Seeing the sheer drop that lay before them, they both began screaming as their craft made its way down the wave. The white fierce water from the crest seemed to remain where it was.

They travelled to the bottom of the wave and began gliding towards the shoreline. The girls stopped screaming and started laughing. They had almost reached land when they heard a tremendous noise. It sounded like a huge waterfall. The girls stopped laughing and looked over their shoulder. They could see the fifty-meter white wall of water travelling towards them. There was a silent pause for a fraction of a second and then, looking at each other once again, they let out a huge scream. The girls continued to scream until their dinghy was finally washed up onto the beach and slowly came to a halt. They sat looking towards the huge wave that was about to wash over them. They had no hope of escaping as they huddled together.

Above the roar of the water, they could hear a high-pitched sound. When they looked down at the shoreline, they could see the dolph-maids frantically swimming up and down in the shallow water. The girls stood up and began waving their arms and shouting at them to get out of the way and to swim to safety. They chose to ignore the girls and continued to swim backwards and forwards up and down the shoreline. They repeated this action over and over again, weaving in and out of each other at tremendous speeds. The girls watched in astonishment as the dolph-maids actions created a wave. The wave travelled along the beachfront from one side to the other. It slowly increased in size until its height was higher than the wave coming from the lake.

Clinging to each other, Freya and Hassina buried their heads in each other's shoulders as a huge dark shadow loomed over them. Gym stood barking defiantly. He lowered his tail and began snarling and baring his teeth at the wall of water. The lake wave reached the shore but the water did not engulf the girls. The force of the dolph-maids wave knocked it sideways. Both waves then swept along the entire stretch of the shoreline and curved around the island. Ecstatic, the girls began dancing and cheering on the sandy beach.

The dolph-maids performed one final display of acrobatics. Freya and Hassina watched as their new friends headed back towards the lake. The girls waved goodbye. They were relieved that their ordeal was over but were sad to be parted from their rescuers.

CHAPTER 10

INCLUSION

It had taken the best part of the day to cross the lake, longer than they had anticipated. The girls considered setting up camp for the night. Suddenly, they both heard the voice of a child in their minds. The voice was urging them onwards. There were still a few more hours of daylight remaining. Both girls agreed that they needed to continue for just a little while longer. At least until there was no light to guide their way.

Ahead of them was a steep rocky mountain. They began the long ascent towards the summit. It was a difficult climb. At times their feet slipped on the loose rocks causing them to slide backwards. Where possible they used the larger rocks protruding out of the mountain to steady themselves.

After climbing for a couple of hours, they finally reached the summit. Freya was the first to reach the top. She could feel a cold breeze on her face. Standing upright, she threw her head back and looked up in amazement at the flame coloured sky. Stretching her arms out to the side and spreading her fingers apart, she could feel the cool air rushing through her hands. Freya began twirling around in circles, elated that she had reached the summit. Her cousin reached the top a few seconds later. Hassina was horrified to see Freya being so conspicuous. She could be exposing their position to the enemy. She grabbed hold of Freya's arm and pulled her to the floor.

Lying flat on the ground, they crawled in commando fashion to the far side of the mountaintop and peered over the edge. It was a long way down. They hung their faces over the vast drop, which caused Freya's head to spin.

As they looked down, they saw another mountain opposite. There were numerous caves carved out of its side. At the entrance to each cave, a shadowy figure paced up and down. Freya hadn't realised they were so close to the Gloamin camp. She was mortified that she may have jeopardised their rescue mission. Hassina was sure they hadn't been detected. However, she stressed they must be more vigilant. If they wanted to avoid being captured, they must be quiet and keep out of sight. Any further communication between the girls was to be spoken in whispers.

In the gorge below was a fortified wooden enclosure. It sat between the two mountains. Hassina sensed this is where Jalay and the children were being held.

They each took turns to keep watch. When darkness finally fell, the Gloamins began to emerge from the caves. Freya whispered to Hassina to come and look at what was happening. They both lay down and stared at the Gloamins for a long time. There were hundreds of them.

Freya was frightened and had misgivings about rescuing the children. She was concerned that the sheer number of Gloamins would make the children's liberation impossible. Even if they did manage to release the children from the enclosure, she was convinced they would be unable to pass the guards. Hassina told Freya there was no need to panic; together they would work everything out. She had a plan. As soon as the sun came up, they would make their way down to the enclosure. This would be the best time to rescue the children. The Gloamins would head for the caves as soon as the sun begins to rise. The creatures would watch the enclosure from the caverns. If the Gloamins did see the children escaping, they would be unable to do anything to stop them. Daylight would be the girl's ally.

This plan sounded fantastic to Freya and should guarantee a trouble free rescue mission. Hassina stressed they were so close. They needed to act sooner rather than later. She didn't know how long it would be before the Gloamins moved their camp elsewhere. They would have to be extremely careful and ensure they remained hidden at all times.

Hassina advised Freya to get some sleep. Freya was too tired to argue. She snuggled down into a sleeping bag. Gym wandered over and lay at her feet.

Hassina took the first watch, continually scanning the enclosure for any sign of Jalay or the children. Unfortunately, the view of the majority of the enclosure was obscured by a thick forest of pine trees that were positioned down the mountainside.

She tried mind speaking but there was no response. They had been unable to hear the voice since they had visual contact with the enclosure. She wondered if the child's voice had been a telepathic echo. This was unlikely. She suspected that something or someone had put up a barrier around the camp preventing any thought exchange.

Freya had rested for a few hours and it was now her turn to observe the camps activities. Hassina woke her gently. Freya wrapped her sleeping bag around her shoulders and watched enviously as Hassina snuggled down and closed her eyes. Gym nestled up beside her and they were both asleep within a few seconds.

Freya crawled to the edge of the gorge. Resting on her elbows, she peered over the ledge, it was pitch black. She found it very difficult to distinguish between the shapes wandering around the camp.

She had an idea. She took the sketchbook out of the backpack and flicked through the pages. When she found what she was looking for, she laid the picture in front of her. Picking up the night vision goggles, she put them on. They were fantastic. Everything looked clearer; it was amazing. The enclosure was dimly lit by burning torches which were placed at intervals all around the walls. The only sign of life were the Gloamins, scurrying like rats around the outer perimeter. Freya shuddered. They gave her the creeps. She thought of poor Jalay and the children and how frightened they must be seeing the horrible creatures up close.

She remembered the voice she had heard in her mind before they began to climb the mountain. The little voice had asked many questions. "Are you near Freya? Are you coming to help us?" Freya had concentrated and heard herself speaking back. She had asked the child's name and discovered he was called Lyoneth. Now darkness had fallen. No matter how hard she concentrated, she could not contact the voice. Her telepathic gifts had deserted her for the moment. She would be so disappointed if they disappeared permanently. She had only just acquired them.

Freya watched the sunrise. It was a beautiful sight. She had never been afraid of the dark. However, since her first encounter with the creatures, she dreaded nightfall in this strange land.

When most of the Gloamins had drifted back into the caves, she woke Hassina. The girls were eager to get started. They needed to use their time wisely. It was essential they utilised the daylight as much as possible if they were to rescue the children.

Hassina suggested they make their way down the left hand side of the mountain. The large wooded area should provide them with adequate camouflage. The element of surprise would be their weapon. Hassina took out the sketchpad and ripped out a picture. Placing it on the ground, she stepped back to admire her handy work. A green two-seated hovercraft appeared in front of them. Freya was elated. She had never been in a hovercraft before. She was, however, a little concerned about the noise the machine would make. Hassina reassured her that the engine would run silently and they should be able to get down to the camp unheard. Freya looked down at the gorge and could see how very steep it was. She was under no illusion that the journey was going to be easy.

The girls decided it would be better to leave Gym behind. They would collect him on the way back. They were worried he may become excited and his barking would alert the Gloamins. Hassina instructed him to stay. Reluctantly, he lay down with his head resting on his paws. He gave a whimper as they prepared to leave. Freya reassured him that they would be back for him.

She climbed into the seat next to Hassina and braced herself. Ahead of them was a steep wooded area. Their journey would be treacherous. They would have to navigate through thick undergrowth and a forest of trees. Freya knew Hassina would have to concentrate very carefully if they were going to get down in one piece. Hassina instructed Freya to put on her safety belt. She reminded her that no matter how scary the ride became, she wasn't to make a sound.

Freya stretched out her arm and snapped off a twig from a small tree beside her. She placed the stick between her teeth. It would act as a reminder if she felt the need to cry out. Freya had seen actors do this in old war films, normally when they were about to have surgery without anaesthetic or pain relief.

Hassina looked at Freya with the stick in her mouth. She raised her eyes and shook her head.

Hassina turned the key to start the hovercraft. The engine purred as quiet as a kitten. The rubber base beneath them ballooned upwards and outwards. There was a whoosh of air. This flattened the grass and flowers around the base of the machine. The hovercraft began to move forward. Freya braced herself. She was tempted to shout "Yahoo!" but was glad she had the twig between her teeth to remind her not to.

The journey was thrilling at first. However, the further down the mountain they travelled, the thicker the foliage became. Hassina found it difficult to navigate. Freya didn't feel secure. Worrying she was going to fall out, she hung onto the safety straps across her chest.

She clenched her teeth on the twig and hoped she wouldn't bite down too hard and break a tooth. Her guardian had spent a fortune on her orthodontic treatment and she would be furious if the work had to be repeated.

They were now a third of the way down the hillside and travelling at tremendous speed. Obstacles appeared in front of them every few seconds. Hassina was a very skilled driver, successfully managing to dart between the trees and bushes.

They had to swerve quickly on several occasions to avoid crashing although there were several near misses.

Closing her eyes reduced Freya's temptation to scream. With her eyes shut, Freya relied on Hassina's instructions to avoid coming into contact with any protruding objects. She would direct Freya to lean left or right and would tell her to duck if there was a low hanging branch. Their technique seemed to be working.

They were three quarters of the way down the hillside when Hassina swerved to avoid hitting a tree. Unfortunately, the side of the hovercraft clipped a large boulder protruding from the ground. The hovercraft then flipped over. Regrettably, Hassina's head came into contact with the forest floor. They travelled upside down for several meters. It finally came to a halt wedged upside down between two trees.

Turning to her cousin, Freya announced that next time she would be doing the driving. She waited for a sarcastic comment but there was just complete silence. She gave Hassina's arm a shake but could not rouse her at all. Freya became worried. She needed to get out of her upturned position and get down to the ground.

She would have to unbuckle her belt and fall the short distance to the floor. She counted down, "three, two, one". Releasing the buckle, Freya tumbled the short distance and landed flat on her back. She lay there for a few seconds. When she had convinced herself that she hadn't broken anything, she got to her feet. Arching her spine, she rubbed the muscular area of her back that had come into contact with the ground. She made her way around to the other side of the tree.

Freya knelt down on the floor under the overturned hovercraft and looked up. Hassina was unconscious. How was she going to get her cousin down without harming her further? Freya had passed her first aid certificate in school. This gave her some basic knowledge of how to treat injured people. She had to get a grip of herself. The reality was she would have to take on the responsibility. There was nobody else. She took a deep breath in and slowly out. Miss Higgins had encouraged the whole class to do this breathing exercise during exam week. It had helped everyone think more clearly and focus. Freya wasn't finding it particularly helpful today.

She needed to examine Hassina more closely, so she decided to climb up the tree. Stretching over, she was able to observe Hassina's breathing. It was shallow but regular. She could feel a rapid weak pulse. Freya had forgotten the significance of this but was glad Hassina was still alive. She gave a huge sigh of relief and began moving onto the next part of her rescue plan.

The backpack was wedged at the front of the hovercraft by Hassina's feet. With several sharp tugs, she managed to retrieve the bag and drop it onto the ground. Jumping out of the tree, she took out the paint book and flicked through the pages, looking for inspiration.

Finally, she found a painting, which she felt was perfect. Freya placed the picture of a blown up air bed under the upturned hovercraft. Once it had become real, she reached up and released the clasp on Hassina's safety belt Freya stood directly underneath the hovercraft with her knees bent and her arms outstretched. Her plan was possibly a little ambitious. Her aim was to catch Hassina as she dropped out of the seat and try to control her landing. Hassina began falling towards the ground and dropped into Freya's arms. Unfortunately, Freya had underestimated Hassina's weight. They both landed onto the airbed in a heap. Hassina let out a moan as she came into contact with Freya. It took a lot of struggling but eventually Freya managed to drag herself from beneath her cousin's body. Once upright, she pushed and pulled Hassina until she was safely in the middle of the bed. Freya then took hold of the straps at one end of the mattress and began dragging it. She needed to get away from the hovercraft just in case it broke free. Freya headed towards flatter ground at the bottom of the hill. It was hard work. The airbed repeatedly became snagged on stones and twigs. This would jolt the mattress to a sudden halt and slowed down the decent on several occasions. When she reached the bottom, she stumbled and fell backwards. Frustrated, she could feel tears welling up in her eyes. She was tired and frightened but determined not to give in. She climbed to her feet and once again began dragging the bed.

Eventually she reached the bottom of the slope. She stopped under the shade of a huge tree and fell to the ground with exhaustion. There was no time for her to rest. She had to make Hassina as comfortable as possible. Freya flicked through the picture book. Making her selection, she lay the picture down on the ground. It was a parasol and a fan. She thought the parasol would provide extra shade and the fan would keep Hassina cool. However, when the picture became real, she noticed it was an electric fan. Disappointed, she flicked the on switch. To her amazement, it worked.

Freya then began examining Hassina. She needed to determine what injuries Hassina had sustained. When she assessed her cousins left arm, Hassina let out a moan. The arm appeared to be in a peculiar position. Freya was sure it was broken. Taking the first aid kit out of the backpack, she pulled out a triangular bandage. Making it into a sling, she placed it onto the affected arm. Freya then tied a knot at the back of Hassina's neck. The sling looked secure. She hoped this would provide enough support for the injured arm.

Hassina had also sustained a head injury. Freya was able to clean the gaping five-centimetre wound on her cousin's forehead with her bottled water. After applying a dressing, she wrapped a bandage around her head. The only thing to do now was to wait. Hassina needed to be kept under close observation until she recovered consciousness.

Freya heard a rustling noise behind her. Turning slowly, she expected to see something ominous lurking there. To her surprise, something leapt into her arms. It was little Gym. Freya was so glad to see him. She hugged him tightly. He was so very excited to see her. He licked her face madly. Gym kept her company. She was desperately worried and Gym was a good listener.

Hassina continued to remain unresponsive. Time was passing and Freya knew the chance to rescue Jalay and the children was slipping by. She had to make a difficult decision. Leave Hassina with Gym or stay and risk not rescuing the captives.

There was no option. She reluctantly chose to go. Hassina needed to get home and Freya had no idea of how to get her there. Jess would know exactly what to do. Freya rolled Hassina on to her side and placed two large boulders behind her to stop her from rolling on to her back. She remembered the importance of this from her first aid course. If Hassina was sick, at least she wouldn't choke on her vomit. Gym had strict instructions not to leave Hassina. He lay down in front of her and rested his head on her body.

Freya gathered her things together and said goodbye to both of them. She was certain that Gym would guard Hassina and never leave her. Freya was frightened at the thought of going on alone. She picked up the backpack. Knowing she was doing the right thing, she began walking towards the Gloamin's camp. Freya trekked cautiously through the trees. Her heart stopped every time she heard a sound. Once at the edge of the forest, she crouched down behind bushes and peered between the leaves. Freya could see the enclosure and the caves quite clearly.

In the mouths of all the caves were several Gloamins who stood watching the camp below. Freya scanned the area. She needed to find a route through to the camp without being seen. She darted about between trees and bushes, carefully selecting the most camouflaged position. When she was almost certain there were no Gloamins looking in her direction, she leapt out from behind the safety of her hiding place and made a dash for the wooden enclosure. Keeping her eyes fixed on the Gloamin lookouts, she finally reached the fortress. Freya stood with her back against the fence. Looking right to left, she couldn't see any sign of activity.

She crouched down and began to rummage in the backpack. Taking the picture book out of the bag, she flicked through the pages. She didn't know what she was looking for but eventually she chose a picture. It was a tunnel. Freya placed the picture on to the fence. A section of the wood promptly disappeared and she found herself staring into a large black hole. It was about a meter off the ground and two meters in diameter. Taking her phone out of the backpack, she shone it into the darkness. The light revealed a very long dark tunnel. It was difficult to comprehend. The thickness of the fence couldn't have been more than half a metre. The tunnel seemed to be two kilometres long. Freya began to doubt her picture choice; she hadn't exactly picked a fast getaway option.

She cautiously climbed up into the tunnel. It was much darker inside than she had originally thought. Freya was extremely nervous. She worried that something or someone was going to jump out and grab her. There was nothing to see except the darkness. She shone the light from her mobile phone wildly around her. Taking a few slow deep breaths, she began to calm down a little. Freya didn't want to be in the dark any longer than she had to be. She was becoming paranoid that something was lurking in the shadows. She could see daylight at the end of the tunnel and quickly raced towards it. She approached the last few meters with caution and stopped short of the exit.

Freya crept towards the opening and peeped her head outside the tunnel. She was saddened to see there were young children in shackles. They were secured to a wooden pole by a lengthy chain. The younger children were sat in a circle with an older child. As the adolescent turned her head, Freya smiled at her familiar face. It was Jalay. She was desperate to be reunited with her sister and had to restrain herself from running over and giving her a big hug.

Freya waited patiently until a group of older children wandered close to the tunnel entrance. Choosing her moment carefully, she stepped out into the compound and cautiously tagged along behind the group. Freya was surprised they hadn't spotted the huge tunnel entrance. When she looked back at the fence, she was horrified to see the entrance was no longer there. She began to panic. How was she going to get everyone to safety if the escape route had vanished? Believing it must be there somewhere she concentrated her gaze. The tunnel entrance became visible to her. It appeared to be camouflaged by a thin haze of fencing. It was an illusion to fool any onlookers. Freya was relieved she still had their escape route in place.

She walked behind the group of children until she was close to Jalay. She then left the group and inched her way towards the circle of younger children.

Freya knelt down and joined the group. Looking at Jalay, she realised she was seeing her sister for the first time. Jalay let out a brief scream of delight. Freya quickly leant forward and slapped her hand over Jalay's mouth. When she had finally calmed down, Freya removed her hand and the two girls hugged. They both began speaking at the same time. They were so excited to see each other.

The noise of the chattering sisters woke Lyoneth. He had been sleeping. The younger children slept very poorly at night due to the Gloamin activity. They normally napped throughout the day. Sleepily, he wandered over to Freya and gave her a big hug. He was so pleased to see her. Lyoneth knew she would come and asked her if she was going to take them home. This was the voice Freya had heard in her head. He sat down beside her and listened intently as the girls talked through the escape plan.

Freya explained what had happened to Hassina and briefly discussed her injuries. Jalay was very concerned and wanted to get back to her cousin as soon as possible.

Jalay asked Freya if she had brought the sketchbook. Freya produced the book from the backpack and handed it to her sister. Jalay flicked through the pages and eventually chose a picture. She tore it out and put it on the ground. The picture became real. Freya looked down and saw a set of bolt cutters. Jalay began calling the younger children to her. She discretely began cutting their chains. She then asked the freed children to sit together against the fence close to the escape tunnel.

It was Freya's job to organise the older children. She ensured they were each responsible for a small group of the younger ones. Freya took responsibility for Lyoneth. When he was released from his shackles, they sidled over to the fence. With a cautious look around, Freya and Lyoneth quickly climbed into the tunnel. They waited just inside the entrance.

Jalay was with the first group. She needed to receive the children at the other end and tell them where to go. Freya and Lyoneth guided the others in to the entrance and encouraged them to hurry through the tunnel. Lyoneth loved being in charge and gave each group a sense of urgency to escape.

The remaining children in the compound were primarily adolescents. They had dispersed themselves around the camp and made themselves obvious to the Gloamin lookouts. This gave the smaller children chance to escape.

Whilst Freya kept watch, the last few teenagers entered the tunnel. She scanned the compound to ensure that no one had been left behind. Unfortunately, as she put her head out of the tunnel she sensed she was being watched. Freya looked up. She could see two Gloamins pointing in her direction. She held her breath for a brief second. Panic rushed through her veins. Then she remembered. The Gloamins were unable to follow them as the sun was still up. Hassina's plan was working. It was then her heart sank.

Two silver robed figures appeared at the cave entrance and looked directly at her. The silver robes started running towards the enclosure. Freya shouted to the children already in the tunnel to run as fast as they could. Lyoneth and Freya held hands and raced after the others.

They were two thirds of the way through the tunnel when Freya heard a noise behind them. Glancing over her shoulder, she could see the silver robed men had entered the tunnel and were chasing them. Freya started running even faster. Poor Lyoneth was pulled along at such a pace he was practically horizontal. The caped figures were a short distance behind them. They were gaining fast. Jalay stood at the exit screaming at Freya and Lyoneth to hurry. She could see the silver robed men getting closer.

On reaching the end of the tunnel, Freya dived through the exit dragging Lyoneth with her. They landed face down on the ground. Lyoneth lay on the floor exhausted. Jalay screeched at Freya to look behind her. Freya who was now on her feet turned to look at the tunnel. The tattooed arm of one of the silver hooded men stretched through the exit and grasped hold of Freya's shoulder.

The two silver robes were still in the tunnel and if the children were going to have any chance of escape, they would need to remain there. Lyoneth and Jalay held onto Freya tightly and following a fierce struggle, Freya was able to unzip her hooded top. The man gave a sharp tug and fell backwards clutching Freya's sweater. The tattooed man bumped into his accomplice and they both crashed to the floor.

Jalay quickly snatched the picture from the wall and scrunched it up, trapping the silver robed men inside. She pushed the scrunched tunnel picture deep into the backpack. Freya questioned her sister's action. Jalay felt they had no alternative. If the picture were discarded, the silver robes would escape and begin their pursuit of the children once again. Freya nodded in agreement. Jalay was right, they had no alternative.

They quickly made their way into the forest to join the others. Jalay carried out a head count to ensure that no one was left behind. When she was happy that everyone was accounted for, they set off in the direction of Freya's first aid post.

The small children ran on ahead enjoying their newfound freedom. On arriving at camp, the girls were overjoyed to see Hassina awake. She was leaning against a rock, obviously in pain but she masked this by greeting them with a big smile.

Gym was excited to see them and weaved in and out of their legs as they walked. The children made a big fuss of him. Unfortunately, they all tried to pet him at the same time. This was a little overwhelming for Gym who ran off, followed closely by the younger children. Jalay cautioned the children not to stray too far. The adolescents managed to gather the younger children together despite their protests. Gym helped by reappearing. The little ones were organised into forming an orderly queue. They took turns in stroking him.

The girls gave Hassina a big hug. She winced. They had forgotten about her painful shoulder. Jalay wanted to get Hassina medical help as soon as possible. She hoped her cousin would be well enough to travel. Poor Hassina would also have the responsibility of getting the children home safely. If she was able to do this, Jalay and Freya would remain behind and try to retrieve the stolen key. The girls had achieved half of their mission; it would be wonderful if they could complete it. They were very aware of the potential consequences if they didn't. Hassina was happy to take on the challenge. The adolescents in the group reassured Jalay that they would all take good care of each other.

Jalay looked through the sketchpad and tore out a picture. She placed it on the ground. A beautifully coloured hot air balloon appeared in front of them. Below the balloon was a huge wicker basket which was large enough to accommodate everyone. Fortunately, it was still daylight. The Gloamins would remain in their caves for several hours. The girls hoped seeing the balloon leave would trick the enemy into thinking all the children had escaped. This would hopefully give Freya and Jalay the element of surprise.

They said their goodbyes and everyone crouched inside the basket. Freya found it very difficult to say goodbye to Lyoneth. They hugged for a long time before he was reassured that they would meet very soon. The balloon left the ground and rose higher and higher. Jalay and Freya looked up and could see the basket climbing up above the trees. There was a sense of relief that Hassina and the children were safely on their way.

CHAPTER 11

AFFIRMATION

The girls walked back towards the first aid post. Jalay put her arm around Freya's shoulder and wanted to know everything that had happened since they were last together.

Freya decided to get her confession out of the way. She became very serious and asked Jalay to sit down. Jalay had to promise not to be cross. Freya had something important to tell her. Jalay was intrigued. They sat down on a log at the edge of the clearing. Freya told Jalay that she knew all about their past and their true relationship. Jalay was surprised. She sat looking at Freya but didn't say anything. When she did eventually speak, she expressed how happy she was not to have to keep the secret any longer. Jalay began to cry. Freya put her arms around her sister and hugged her.

Jalay tried to explain why she hadn't told Freya previously. Freya told Jalay that it didn't matter and that the most important thing was that they were together. They would now share all their hopes, dreams and fears. Jalay couldn't help thinking that her little sister was obviously maturing and how right she had been to invite her along on their adventure.

The darkness was beginning to creep in around them. Both girls had the same thought. The Gloamins would be starting to wander around very soon. The girls needed to have a plan if they were going to retrieve the key. Jalay had many skills she wished to pass on to Freya.

Turning to her sister, she asked her if she would like a flying lesson. Freya said she had always fancied flying a helicopter. Jalay pulled a disapproving face and shook her head. She decided it might be better to demonstrate. Jalay asked Freya to watch her carefully. She leapt up from the log and began running across the clearing. She jumped with both feet together, with her knees slightly bent and sprang up into the air. Instead of falling back down to the ground, she began climbing upwards through the sky. Jalay was moving her arms and legs in circular movements. It looked like the breaststroke swimming technique. Freya swam like this at home but instead of pushing water out of the way to move forward, Jalay appeared to be moving air. When she felt she had gained enough height, she began turning and twisting in different directions. Freya looked up in amazement as Jalay continued to soar around the sky. Satisfied with her demonstration, she floated down to the ground, slowly and gracefully. She then patiently explained to Freya the basic techniques of this new skill. Jalay's most important piece of advice was for Freya to have confidence in herself; she was a Ledremain.

All their citizens possessed the skills to fly. It was the same principal as learning to swim in a swimming pool. The ability to believe that you can float must be utmost in your mind.

Freya was excited and wanted to get up into the sky straight away. Her first attempt, however, did not go completely to plan. She ran across the clearing, put her feet together, and bent her knees. Unfortunately, her right foot landed in a small rabbit hole causing her ankle to buckle underneath her and she tumbled to the ground. Unperturbed, she dusted herself down and began again. On her second attempt, she managed to get off the ground. However, when Freya became aware of her weightlessness, she panicked. In her attempt to stop herself from falling, she waved her arms up and down like a bird flapping its wings. Unfortunately, this didn't help. Freya started plummeting towards the ground, screaming as she fell. Jalay then took control of the situation by extending her arms out in front of her. She then placed one hand on top of the other. With her palms facing upwards, she moved them around in a circular anti-clockwise motion. Her actions appeared to suspend Freya in mid air, causing her to hover one meter above the ground. Freya was thrilled. Now calm and relaxed, she lay in the air with her hands behind her head and her legs crossed. She glanced at her sister and smiled. She was then able to turn over onto her front and begin moving her arms and legs in a circular motion. Eventually, she gained more confidence and began swimming higher. Jalay joined Freya and whilst they were in the air, she was able to demonstrate other flying techniques.

Another method was speed flying. This was more difficult and required the use of the front crawl technique. Jalay kept her legs straight and kicked her feet up and down like a pair of flippers. Her arms moved in a forward, overhead stroke position. Freya tried this but complained that she found this technique very tiring.

Jalay then moved on to the next lesson which was how to land safely. On the first few occasions, Freya had several bumpy landings, resulting in minor cuts and bruises. This prompted her to master the landing skills very quickly. It had been a successful tutorial. Jalay felt they were as prepared as they could possibly be.

The girls waited until it was pitch black and then made their way towards the Gloamin's camp. When they reached the enclosure, they hid themselves behind some large bushes which were next to the perimeter fence. They were able to squat down and observe the activities in the camp through a small gap between the wooden posts. Their objective was to locate and retrieve the stolen key. The girls suspected it would be in the camp. They had to be very patient and wait for an opportune moment to retrieve it.

The Gloamins had started to make their way out of the caves. They were gathering in the large open area within the wooden enclosure. The creatures stood together looking upwards, their eyes transfixed on the moon. The girl's attention was drawn away from the enclosure momentarily as they discussed tactics. Suddenly, there was a deafening explosion. Freya peeped through the fence she could see the camp gates had been destroyed. In their place were six silver-cloaked figures. The Gloamins greeted the mysterious strangers with a raucous cheer. They brandished their weapons above their heads. Some merely held wooden staffs but others had swords and spears.

Their silver robed masters walked through the sea of Gloamins towards an elevated platform at the far end of the enclosure. It was difficult for the girls to see their faces. They were hidden in the shadows of their hooded robes. The shrouded figures climbed the wooden steps leading up to the platform and turned to face the Gloamin spectators.

The most senior cloaked figure wore a silver robe edged in aquamarine precious stones. He spoke to the Gloamins, promising them power to rule the earth lands. He told them that the missing keys had to be found and they must be prepared to destroy anything in their path to retrieve them. Their reward would be a new homeland for their nation. The words fuelled their frenzy and they began shrieking and yelling excitedly.

The silver robes then formed a circle. Raising their arms, they placed their hands palm to palm and chanted loudly. The most senior silver robe raised his voice above the others. He then recited an incantation in a strange tongue. The language was unfamiliar to Freya. She found it frustrating that she couldn't understand what was being said. She turned to Jalay for guidance but she simply shook her head and shrugged her shoulders. Jalay knew it was the old language of Ledremain. She hadn't heard it spoken for thirteen years and had forgotten the old teachings. She could only understand an occasional word but she did tell Freya to be prepared to move swiftly.

The Gloamins now joined in the chanting. They made a shrieking sound which was distressing to the girls and they were forced to put their fingers in their ears. The girls continued to watch in amazement.

The circle of cloaked figures began to rise up at least two meters from the floor. They moved around palm to palm in an anti-clockwise direction. As they did so, the floor of the platform opened up like a flower. Gradually a mist appeared around them and there was a bright flash of light. Suddenly, they stopped moving and hovered in the air. The cloaked figures then slowly drifted down onto the platform. They continued to stand with their hands palm to palm.

A large arch shaped window ascended from deep below the ground. It floated up to the platform spinning around in a clockwise direction. Brilliant coloured flashing lights were projected from the window across the enclosure. The light was so dazzling; it was hard for the girls to focus and continue watching. The brightness intensified, forcing the Gloamins to cower close to the ground and cover their eyes.

When the light subsided, the girls could see the window had stopped spinning. It slowly floated down settling at the rear of the platform. The window was approximately three meters high and two meters wide. The girls could see a huge blue oval shaped eye in its centre.

The senior robed figure held a wooden box in the air. The box had a gold key with a sparkling emerald on its handle. When the cloaked figure lifted the lid, a bright light engulfed him. The light shot out of the box and immediately entered the edges of the window making it glow. The silver robe then dropped the box and held the key up in the air.

At that moment, Jalay sprang to her feet. It was time to act. Freya stumbled to her feet but Jalay was already away. She watched as her sister ran along the side of the enclosure. Bringing her feet together and slightly bending her knees, she jumped off the ground. Jalay began moving her arms and legs through the black sky. Freya took a deep breath and followed. She was astounded that she had managed to get up into the air on her first attempt. All she had to do was concentrate and focus on not falling.

In the enclosure, the silver robed senior figure stepped forward from the circle. With arms outstretched, he waved the key to the crowds of Gloamins. Their piercing screams filled the air. The hooded figure then walked towards the window.

The girls swam over the fence and made their way towards the platform. They flew three metres above the heads of the creatures and were about ten meters away from the window. The girls held their breath hoping to remain undetected. They were now swimming alongside each other. The plan was to swoop down and grab the key from the hand of the silver robe. If Jalay failed, Freya was to make one attempt only to retrieve the key. She should then escape over the fence to safety.

As they approached the platform, Jalay adjusted her flight path and was now only one meter above the Gloamin's heads. She started speed flying towards the window. Freya had mastered the slower stroke. She was not very confident in her speed swimming ability. She was tempted to try it once again but thought better of it. Slow but sure, as her mum would often tell her.

Jalay could see the senior silver robe was reaching forward to put the key into the window lock. Jalay's arm was out-stretched. She made a grab for the key. Unfortunately, she missed but did manage to knock the key out of the senior robe's hand. The key began falling to the floor. Freya seized the opportunity to swoop down with her hand open and palm facing upwards. She managed to catch the key and turned to swim away. Suddenly one of the robed figures grabbed hold of her leg and the force of the jolt caused Freya to drop the key.

Holding onto her leg, the silver robed figure swung her around and then let go. She was now catapulting through the air. Freya tried to recover the control of her flying but it was futile. She collided with the fence. The impact caused dreadful pain in her back. She eventually slumped to the ground.

When she looked up, she could see the senior silver robed figure had picked up the key. The key was then pushed into the window lock. Jalay made a second attempt to retrieve the key. She swooped down but two of the silver robed men wrestled her to the floor. She was now held firmly by her arms.

The senior turned the key in the lock and pushed the window. As the window opened, the brightness disappeared. Jalay could see the world beyond. It was a bleak, dark and desolate place. The silver robes passed her to the nearest Gloamins who now gripped her firmly. Jalay remembered their grip from the cave. Their sharp talons dug into her arm. She could hear her skin breaking and could feel blood trickling down her arms. She watched as the hooded figures disappeared through the window into the blackness.

The senior silver robed figure ordered the Gloamins to follow with their prisoners. Two of the Gloamins made their way towards Freya. She sprang to her feet. Freya had only just escaped the silver robe's clutches. She wasn't about to become one of their prisoners. Before the Gloamins could reach her, Freya ran forward and leapt into the air. She snatched a lit torch from the fence. Flying towards Jalay, she noticed how hysterical the Gloamins had become. They were frantically pushing and shoving as they made their way towards the window. Jalay and Freya sensed the atmosphere and feared something dreadful was about to happen. Freya swam towards Jalay. On reaching her, she swung the torch she was holding and hit one of the Gloamins in the face. Then, turning sharply in the air, she flew back. Swinging the torch once again, she hit the second Gloamin. This stunned the creature. Freya took the opportune moment to swoop down and grab hold of Jalay by the waist. Soaring high into the air, they flew to safety. The girls were now flying side by side.

When they looked down, they could see all the Gloamins were fighting to get through the window. It was as if they knew something terrible was going to happen. Freya had a feeling that something was wrong. They needed to get out of there as quickly as possible. Jalay pointed to a cliff top in the distance. She felt they would be safe there. Freya nodded in agreement and followed Jalay. On reaching the top of the mountain, they were able to look down at the enclosure.

The girls noticed the window was beginning to close. The Gloamins had now become even more frantic than before and were fighting each other as they forced their way through the opening. The piercing screams of the Gloamins could be heard from the top of the mountain.

Despite their distance from the window, the girls sensed they were still in danger. Freya suggested they swam away. Jalay explained that because of Freya's inexperience, she would be unable to fly too far. Jalay rummaged in the backpack for the sketchpad. She put a picture down on the ground in front of them. A great big fluffy white cloud appeared. Jalay was about to step on it when Freya pulled her back. She was not confident the cloud would support their weight. She had visions of them slipping through and falling on to the sharp rocks below. Jalay tried to reassure Freya that it would be safe. Ignoring Freya's fears, Jalay promptly jumped onto the cloud. She turned and held her hand out to Freya, telling her not to be scared. Freya could see that Jalay's weight was supported but would it hold the two of them? Freya cautiously stepped onto the cloud. It was bouncy just like a trampoline. Freya started jumping up and down until Jalay told her to stop. The cloud speedily made its way upwards. They could hear the wind whistling past their ears. Exhausted, they lay down to rest. In no time at all, they were asleep.

CHAPTER 12

REUNION

The bright sunrise woke them the following morning. In the distance, they could see the outline of the cloud city buildings. They approached the palace and were thrilled to see the hot air balloon docked in front of them. Freya and Jalay hoped Hassina and the children had all arrived safely.

The cloud stopped at the palace pathway. They disembarked and were greeted by Romain. He introduced himself to Freya and reminded her that they had met when she was a small baby. Freya thanked him for saving her life. She was grateful for everything he had done to protect her. Romain felt no thanks were necessary and it had been a pleasure to assist the family. His only regret was that he had been unable to help their mother and father.

Romain led the girls through the entrance hall of the palace. He then opened the door to a very large room packed with people. They were all chatting but as soon as Freya and Jalay entered the room, there was rapturous applause. The rescued children had been reunited with their parents and were all very happy to see Freya and Jalay arrive safely. Everyone stepped forward to shake their hands and thank them. Freya eagerly scanned the crowd for signs of Lyoneth. She couldn't see him and assumed his parents must have already collected him. She was sad she hadn't had chance to say goodbye.

Romain put his hands around their shoulders and escorted them to Hassina. They were taken to a hospital room occupied by doctors and nurses dressed in white uniforms. Patients lay in silver framed hospital beds with white linen sheets. It was a pristine environment. The girls stood at the bottom of Hassina's bed, watching her sleep. She looked very peaceful. Although it was a struggle, she succeeded in opening her eyes for a brief moment. Hassina smiled, closed her eyelids once again, and drifted off to sleep.

Romain ushered them out of the room. He explained that Hassina's arm had required an operation. Because of the procedure, she would be unable to carry out any strenuous activity for several weeks. The girls were reassured that Romain and his team of experts would take good care of her.

Romain led the girls through to another room. There was an open fire in the centre. With loud sighs of contentment, they slumped down onto a large comfortable white couch. The girls then recounted their adventure to Romain. He was full of praise at their bravery and realised what a tremendous ordeal this had been for them. He was convinced they were going to need additional help. Romain was certain, if they were to stand any chance of retrieving the other keys, they must develop more of their powers. He was positive that they could not do that on an empty stomach. He laughed and promptly organised refreshments. The food was served on silver platters and placed on a low table in front of them. There was a variety of fruits and some tasty looking pastries. The girls had no hesitation in tucking in.

Whilst they were eating, there was a knock at the door. A tall young man entered, smiling. Jalay let out a scream and leapt to her feet. Running over to him, she threw her arms around his neck shouting his name. The young man swung her round laughing. When he finally put Jalay down, she took hold of his hand and pulled him over to the couch where they stood in front of Freya. Jalay introduced the young man as Sithe. Freya stood up to greet her brother. He hugged her. His embrace made her feel secure and she began to sob.

In the past, Wes had always been the one to support her. Freya relied upon him to give her a hug when her earth parents were being unreasonable. Her earth mother and father had rarely shown her affection. Since embarking on her journey, she understood why. Sithe made her feel that everything would be okay from now onwards. When she had stopped sobbing, he put her at arm's length. Holding one of her hands, he twirled her around. He was in his early twenties, although he looked younger. He had dark curly hair and deep green eyes. He was a very handsome young man. Freya knew he would make sure she was protected. Suddenly the door was flung open. Lyoneth charged in and ran over to Freya giving her a hug. Sithe then introduced Lyoneth as the youngest member of their family. The girls were ecstatic.

Freya could not believe her good fortune. Not only had she discovered a sister but she had found two brothers as well. Freya had so many questions she wanted to ask.

Sithe described the events that took place thirteen years ago on Ledremain. Their father had told him to cut the rope. It was attached to the boat carrying the girls. He described how he had watched the boat drift across the red smoked filled sky. He had never forgotten that night. He had felt guilty about the part he had played. Not knowing if the girls were dead or alive had haunted his dreams. Sithe and their parents had mounted their Similies and followed the boat until it had completely disappeared. The three of them had travelled from village to village searching for the girls for many months. The Gloamin patrols were everywhere. It was unsafe to remain on Ledremain.

Edmortar decided to take his wife and son away from the immediate danger. They settled on a planet called Daluce. The girls were never forgotten. Their names were spoken every evening before supper. Tears welled up in Sithe's eyes as he re-lived the memories. Freya hugged him and whispered "well we are here now". Sithe smiled.

Romain was delighted that they were now a group of four. When their cousin recovered from her injuries, they would be five. Together Romain felt they would be invincible. Freya was unconvinced and doubted the group's chances against such formidable opponents. What could four people do against the sheer numbers and experience of their adversaries? Jalay agreed with Freya. She felt it was pure luck that they had survived up to now. They may not be as fortunate in their future pursuit of the keys. Lyoneth was more positive. He felt that, together, they would be amazing. He was certain that the four of them would be successful in retrieving the next key. Sithe nodded.

The girls were keen to hear news of their parents. Sithe was sorry he didn't have anything positive to say. He had been unable to find their mother and father following the Gloamin attack on Daluce. They had become separated during the battle. He had been with his father and a group of elders when the fighting had begun. Edmortar had instructed Sithe and some of the elders to make their way to the west side of the village. There was a high concentration of Gloamins attacking the barricades and only a small number of warriors defending. Their father and the rest of the group went to the aid of their mother Sapera. The fighting spread to different sections of the village and continued until daybreak when the Gloamins finally retreated.

Sithe searched for Lyoneth and his parents. He assumed they had all escaped to the forest but there was no sign of them. He believed when peace was restored, their parents would return. Lyoneth sat down, put his hands over his face, and began to cry. His brother and sisters could hear his thoughts and feel his pain. Freya comforted him. Everyone realised they had to continue. They had to stop the Gloamins causing any more misery. People were depending upon them. They had to get to the next key before the creatures. With Romain's help they would formulate a plan.

Romain suggested they return to the attic. He felt this might help them organise their thoughts. After some discussion, they decided to take Romain's advice. They said goodbye to the sleeping Hassina as they wondered how they would manage without her.

Romain escorted them to their transport at the end of the pathway. Freya was amazed to see four seats waiting for them. She wondered how the chair keeper knew they required four seats and not three as before. Romain merely smiled, amused by her question.

The brothers and sisters sat down on the chairs. Lyoneth was very excited and began fidgeting. The girls sat him on the seat between them and fastened his safety belt. Lyoneth did surprise the others by remaining seated throughout the entire journey. He became hypnotised by his surroundings.

Jalay explained to Sithe and Lyoneth about her imminent change of appearance once they enter the attic. They seemed to take the news in their stride.

The group soared above the clouds and finally passed through the attic ceiling. The chairs then settled in the middle of the room. Lyoneth unfastened his safety belt and jumped off his seat. He was excited and began exploring.

Whilst the others chatted, Lyoneth examined the various wall paintings. He called to Freya. She walked over to him curious to hear what he had to say. He expressed his dislike of one of Jalay's paintings. Her youngest brother stood in front of what remained of the green wall picture. It was now a black and desolate scene. It was as if a huge explosion had taken place and destroyed everything in its path. There were many dead Gloamins lying on the floor of a burnt forest. It was a horrific apocalyptic scene. Freya called to Jalay and Sithe. She wanted their opinion. They all stared at the painting. The girls now understood why the Gloamins had been frantic to get through the window. Once the window was unlocked, there was obviously a very short time to pass through to the other dimension before a huge explosion occurred. The girls had sensed the danger as they waited to escape on their cloud picture. Everyone was horrified. This scene reminded them of the potential dangers they may face.

Sithe was worried about the hazards that lay ahead and was not happy for Lyoneth to travel with them. The girls disagreed. They were a family and they should stay together. Jalay was positive that between the three of them, they could manage to keep Lyoneth out of trouble. Eventually, the girls persuaded Sithe to allow their little brother to accompany them. The question was, "Where would they begin?" They must plan their next adventure with care and try to anticipate the Gloamins next move. It was essential they locate the second key. The girls looked to Sithe for guidance. He was the eldest and had been dealing with the Gloamins the longest. Freya hoped he would know how to defeat them.

Sithe spoke once again about the night the Gloamins attacked Daluce. His ketarian instructor was known as Eido and was one of the senior elders present that night. They had fought beside each other during those dark hours on Daluce. Sadly, Eido had died in Sithe's arms. As he lay dying, he told Sithe that if the keys were taken, many nations would be destroyed and their citizens enslaved. He foretold that Sithe would be called upon to defend the seekers of the keys. Sithe would be a defender and a follower and it would be another who would lead him. He knew he would be unable to make any decisions about the next part of their journey. He would, however, be there to defend and support any decisions made by their guide. Eido didn't tell him who the key finder would be. However, he did tell Sithe that whoever was chosen would be able to hear the call of the keys.

The group turned to look at Jalay, as she seemed the obvious choice. Jalay had an idea. Perhaps if she stood in front of each of the pictures in turn, she would hear the keys call to her.

Standing in front of the desert picture, she waited patiently. When nothing happened, she was encouraged by the others to move on to the next wall. It was a picture of the sea. She tried concentrating harder but there wasn't even a whisper. Finally, she stood in front of the white wall. She cleared her mind and held her ear to the wall but she heard nothing. Shrugging her shoulders, she took her place with the others. Jalay concluded she was not destined to lead. They knew it definitely wasn't Sithe unless the prediction given by Eido was wrong. Jalay gave Sithe a nudge and told him to stand in front of each of the pictures. Sithe thought it unlikely but was prepared to try. He would need to concentrate. Jalay looked at Lyoneth and smiled. She hoped it would be Sithe who would guide their way. He was the grown up of their group. Unfortunately, he was unsuccessful.

It was now Lyoneth's turn. He didn't hear the keys and asked Jalay what type of sound they made. Poor Lyoneth was very disappointed. Jalay and Sithe however were very relieved that their little brother wouldn't have the responsibility of leading their group.

It was Freya's turn. She stood in the middle of the attic and closed her eyes. A few seconds passed by and the others watched as her hair gradually turned white. Freya had obviously inherited their mother's mood changing hair.

Freya was experiencing a frightening vision. She could see men in silver robes stood in front of an army of Gloamins. Millions of earth people were in chains surrounded by desolation and devastation. Freya was very disturbed by the vision. She carefully blocked out Lyoneth from her thoughts but allowed the others to see her apparition. Sithe spoke to the girl's minds. He immediately tried to reassure them that this was only an insight to what may happen if they were unsuccessful. Their success would ensure the vision would not become a reality. Freya knew he was right. Her hair changed back to its original colour.

Freya closed her eyes once again and her thoughts drifted over each of the painted scenes. She was drawn to the snow scene and stood in front of it. Freya heard the word, "Easeldyne". She turned to the others and repeated the word. She hoped they would give her suggestions of what this may mean. Unfortunately, they shook their heads. Freya turned to face the wall and concentrated once again. She opened her mind. "Easeldyne is an elder and he's somewhere in this painting". The others nodded their heads. Freya was their guide for their second adventure. They would have to trust her instinct even though she was the least experienced in the group and her skills were not yet developed, Freya promised to be brave. She desperately wanted to succeed. Jalay instructed them all to wrap up warm. They were heading for cold climates.

THE END OF BOOK ONE

#0065 - 140716 - C0 - 210/148/9 - PB - DID1516031